EMERGENCY ON THE TRAIL

Phil pointed to a slow gray ribbon that wound itself through the green fields below. "That's the Silverado River," he said to Hollie.

"It's fantastic," she said. But she didn't sound right. The words came out slowly and painfully, as if she had to force them.

"Are you okay?" Stevie asked.

Hollie didn't respond at first. Instead she was taking shallow breaths that didn't seem to satisfy her.

"I'm fine!" Hollie said, and from the way she said it, with a toss of her head, Stevie knew that she was trying to raise a laugh. But there was nothing to laugh at, because Hollie had turned pale with faint blue shadows under her eyes.

"Can you hear me?" Stevie shouted. "Hollie!"

Hollie focused on her and whispered, "Yes." It came out as a horrible wheezing sound. . . .

The Saddle Club series by Bonnie Bryant; ask your bookseller for titles you have missed:

THE SADDLE CLUB

HORSE TRADE

BONNIE BRYANT

BANTAM BOOKS
TORONTO · NEW YORK · LONDON · SYDNEY · AUCKLAND

I would like to thank Mary Kay Tobin, M.D., and Bruce H. Koenig, D.V.M., whose patient explanations about allergies were invaluable to me in writing this book.
I would also like to thank Katie Cooke, who inspired it.

THE SADDLE CLUB: HORSE TRADE
A BANTAM BOOK 0 553 40767 8

First published in USA by Bantam Skylark Books
First publication in Great Britain

PRINTING HISTORY
Bantam edition published 1995

With thanks to Chris and Sam of Coltspring Riding School for
their help in the preparation of the cover.

Bantam Books are published by Transworld Publishers Ltd,
61–63 Uxbridge Road, Ealing, London W5 5SA,
in Australia by Transworld Publishers (Australia) Pty Ltd,
15–25 Helles Avenue, Moorebank, NSW 2170,
and in New Zealand by Transworld Publishers (NZ) Ltd,
3 William Pickering Drive, Albany, Auckland.

Printed and bound in Great Britain by
Cox & Wyman Ltd, Reading, Berkshire

I would like to express my special thanks to Helen Geraghty for her help in the writing of this book.

STEVIE LAKE LOOKED around suspiciously at the audience at the high-school auditorium where the Willow Creek Community Theater staged its productions. Was that man in a tweed coat a hotshot Broadway producer? Was the woman with a deep suntan a Hollywood scout? Would this be the last time that the members of The Saddle Club would be together?

When her song ended, Lisa Atwood lowered her arms, and the auditorium was silent for a second. Then the audience erupted into applause.

"To think we know her," Carole Hanson said as she and Stevie sprang to their feet.

"Maybe she'll send us an autographed picture from time

to time," Stevie said. "Maybe we'll glimpse her on the cover of *People* magazine."

"We can look at her pictures during Saddle Club meetings," Carole said sadly.

For some time Lisa, Carole, and Stevie had been spending every minute of their spare time together, riding horses and helping each other solve problems. Lately, after Lisa had landed the lead role in *Annie*, Stevie and Carole had worried that their friend would forget about The Saddle Club and riding at Pine Hollow, and spend all her time on acting.

"Bravo," the audience shouted as the curtain fell. The crowd stood and began stampeding toward the stage door. The local theater's production of *Annie* had been a giant hit, and Lisa herself had been a megahit.

By the time the girls finished battling through the crowd and had reached the dressing room where the actors were meeting their public, Carole's black hair was escaping from her headband, and her silver Saddle Club pin was crooked. Meanwhile Stevie was rubbing her elbow. A man had zonked her on the arm with his briefcase.

But Lisa was totally composed, smiling under her red Annie wig, and looking totally adorable in her red Annie dress.

Stevie put her arms around Lisa and hugged her. "You were fantastic."

Carole joined the hug. "You were great in last week's dress rehearsal," she added, "but this afternoon you were astounding. The Saddle Club is proud of you."

Lisa sighed and suddenly looked sad, which was the last thing Carole expected.

"What's the matter?" Carole said. "You got three standing ovations and you feel sad?"

"It's over," Lisa said. "This Sunday matinee is the last performance." Lisa looked so miserable that Carole and Stevie had to laugh.

"It looks like you think there's no life after *Annie*," Carole said. "What about The Saddle Club?"

"Remember how you missed us?" Stevie joked. "Remember how you used to save as many as three or four minutes for us at a time?" During rehearsals for *Annie*, Lisa had gotten a little carried away with scheduling herself and organizing her time. She was always efficient and very self-disciplined, but this time she had started scheduling four-minute meetings with her best friends so that she could do two things that were important to her: rehearse for *Annie* and prepare for a Pony Club rally at Pine Hollow Stables. Finally Carole and Stevie had realized Lisa needed their help. They suggested that Lisa become stable manager for the Horse Wise team instead of ride in the rally, and that had helped her concentrate on *Annie*. In the weeks since then, Carole and Stevie had been looking forward to spending more time with Lisa.

"I mean, I knew *Annie* would be over," Lisa went on, "but now it's *really* over, if you see what I mean."

For the usually clear-headed and precise Lisa, who always got straight A's, this was such a muddled thing to say that Stevie and Carole exchanged worried looks.

"Don't you miss Prancer?" Stevie said, referring to the beautiful Thoroughbred at Pine Hollow Stables that Lisa had been working with. "Forget Prancer," Stevie wailed a second later. "Don't you miss us?"

"You know I do," Lisa said. "Actually, I've been counting the days." She pulled off her red wig and said, "I'm going riding tomorrow." And with that she burst into the first line of the famous song from *Annie*, "Tomorrow."

"I hate to tell you this," Carole said, "but even big stars have to go to school. And tomorrow is Monday, and so far as I know, Willow Creek Junior High is planning to be open tomorrow, and Monday is always a monster homework night."

"So I'll go riding in Max's class on Tuesday. That is, if I remember how to ride," Lisa said with a grin.

Max Regnery was the manager of Pine Hollow Stables, where the girls rode, and also their riding instructor.

"I hate to tell you this," Stevie said, "but some people have fright wigs. You, on the other hand, have fright hair."

Lisa turned to look at herself in the mirror and saw that her brown hair, which had been flattened under the wig, was now sticking up in stiff spikes. "Hey," she said, pulling at one of the spikes. "I may have a new career as a punk rocker."

"Don't quit your day job," said Stevie, smiling at the thought of the neat, responsible Lisa suddenly becoming a rock star.

"I don't know about that. Lisa has a lot of talent, and she can do just about anything she wants," said the girl next to Lisa at the makeup table. She was Hollie Bright, Lisa's best friend in the cast of *Annie*. Now Hollie looked like a weird white monster because she had covered her face with cold cream.

"Who's this?" Stevie said. "The Abominable Snowperson?"

"Very funny, Stevie," Hollie said. "You'd better get your makeup off right away, Lisa. Pancake makeup can really wreck your skin. I know from experience that if I don't take it off right away, I break out in blotches."

"Okay," Lisa agreed, turning in one of the canvas chairs to face the makeup mirror. She dipped two fingers into an industrial-size jar of cold cream and sat looking at herself, the glob of cold cream only inches from her face. "Good-bye, Annie," she said to her face in the mirror. "Good-bye, stardom." She looked behind her at a couple of orphans who were taking off their rags, and at Daddy Warbucks, who was stripping off his bald pate, revealing a full head of hair underneath. The play was definitely over. She hated to see the actors turn back into ordinary people.

Lisa looked over at Hollie, who was carefully wiping around her nose with a piece of tissue. Hollie went to Lisa's school, Willow Creek Junior High, and they had kind of known each other before, but when Lisa had joined the cast at Willow Creek Community Theater, they had become fast friends. Hollie, who'd had lots of acting, dancing, and singing lessons—and plenty of stage experience—had been Lisa's "stage coach," teaching her the meaning of strange theatrical terms like "torch carrier." Now that the play was over, Lisa was disappointed that she wouldn't be seeing as much of the other girl.

Suddenly she had an inspiration.

"Why don't you come riding with us, Hollie?" Lisa asked eagerly. "Pine Hollow has lots of horses, and I'm sure Max can find one that's right for you." Max was an ace at helping new riders.

Hollie looked over at her gratefully, and Lisa guessed

that she must have been suffering from an after-show let-down, too.

"I'm not a total beginner," Hollie said, applying a fresh layer of cold cream to her face. "I had lessons for a couple of years when I was eight or nine."

Knowing that Hollie had a knack for dancing, and that she was a fast learner, Lisa figured that she had the potential to be an excellent rider. The first time Lisa went riding at Pine Hollow Stables, she had expected to be a total flop, but she had managed to stay on her horse and even ride half-decently, because she'd had years of ballet lessons.

"So why did you give up riding?" Lisa asked. "I bet you were terrific."

Hollie shrugged. "The demands of my art, darling," she joked. "My Muse was jealous. She wouldn't let me ride."

"The next class is on Tuesday," Stevie said to Hollie. "Get your mother to call Max Regnery to make arrangements. It's lots of fun. You'll already know the three of us."

"I'm not sure I even remember how to mount a horse," Hollie admitted.

"You face the horse's tail, take the reins, and grasp the horse's mane with your left hand, and then you reach for the stirrup with your right. You put your foot in the stirrup and reach with your right hand for the saddle," said Carole.

Stevie and Lisa exchanged grins. Once again Carole had launched into a major lecture on a topic involving horses. Their friend could never resist a chance to share all the things she knew, because she loved horses so much, and she simply assumed that everyone shared her enthusiasm. Carole was the most experienced member of The Saddle Club. She had even been an assistant to Judy Barker, Pine Hollow's veterinarian.

"I know, I know!" Hollie cried, holding up a hand to halt Carole's explanation. Lisa had already clued her in to Carole's tendency to act like a professor of horse-ology. "I just mean that it's been a while."

"Lisa only started riding recently," Carole said. "You wouldn't believe how quickly she's learned. Dedication and concentration are essential. I have a couple of books I could lend you."

"A truck will pull up to your house tomorrow," Stevie joked.

"Okay," Hollie said. "Now I can't wait till Tuesday. I envy you guys so much. You always have something to talk about."

"Horses!" Stevie said. "Is there anything else? I mean, what do other people talk about?"

"Listen," Lisa said, "I've got a great idea. Why don't we

go over to TD's and talk about horses? I know Hollie likes it." TD's was the Tastee Delight Ice Cream Parlor at the local shopping center, and the place where The Saddle Club most frequently held Saddle Club meetings.

"Best of all, we'll be able to see what kind of mind-boggling concoction Stevie orders," Hollie said. Last time Stevie had ordered a sundae with fifteen ingredients, which must have been a record for TD's.

"We'll fill you in on the horses at Pine Hollow," Carole said.

"You showed me the ropes in the theater," Lisa said, putting her arm through Hollie's. "Now it's only fair I show you the ropes at Pine Hollow Stables—the lead rope, the tether. . . ."

Stevie groaned. "I'm going to miss this fantastic discussion."

"You're not coming?" Hollie said, looking disappointed.

"I'd love to," Stevie said. "But I promised Phil I'd do something else."

Phil Marsten was Stevie's boyfriend. He was a rider at Cross County Stables, which was about a half hour away from Pine Hollow.

Carole's eyes twinkled. "Oh, yeah?"

Stevie blushed. "He invited me for dinner and then to go for a trail ride with his Pony Club," she replied. "This may be the last nice fall weekend, so we're taking advantage of it."

"Poor you!" Carole said sarcastically. "Riding under a harvest moon. It sounds practically unbearable."

"It's rough," Stevie said, her blue eyes gleaming. "But someone's got to do it."

"IT's THE BIGGEST moon I ever saw," Stevie said to Phil as she stared dreamily at the red harvest moon hanging over the trees in the darkening sky. The Marstens had just finished dinner, and now Stevie and Phil were walking toward the Marstens' stable.

"The moon always appears bigger when it's close to the earth," said Phil. With his head tipped back to see the moon, and his green eyes shining, Phil looked even more handsome than usual, Stevie thought.

"How come?" she asked.

"Because you can see its huge size compared to things on earth, like trees, or the weather vane on top of the stable." Phil pointed to the vane on top of the Marstens'

11

stable. It was in the shape of a galloping horse, and in the light of early evening the horse on the vane seemed to be galloping directly toward the big red moon.

"I don't mean to bring up a sore subject," said Stevie, looking up at the moon, "but is Teddy spooked by a full moon?" She was remembering that on the last Mountain Trail Overnight, or MTO, Phil's horse, Teddy, had been spooked by almost everything. Teddy was a great horse in the ring or the barn. He was a handsome bay gelding with plenty of power and finesse. But he could be a real wild card out on the trail, and tonight, under a full moon, with the forest full of strange shapes . . . She didn't like to think about it.

"No problem," Phil said. "Mr. Baker told me how to cure Teddy of the spooks." Mr. Baker was the owner and riding instructor at Cross County Stables. "He said that Teddy had a phobia, which is like an allergy of the mind."

Stevie nodded. "I know about phobias. My brother Chad claims he has homework phobia, which prevents him from getting the A's he feels he's entitled to."

Phil grinned. "Sounds logical. I'm not sure I can cure homework phobia, but Mr. Baker's prescription for Teddy worked. I took him out at sunset in small doses—at first five minutes, then ten minutes, building up to longer periods."

"How did Teddy feel about this?" Stevie asked. "I can't imagine he liked being part of a scientific experiment."

Phil shrugged. "I think Teddy understood. He doesn't want to be left behind when I go on trail rides, so he figured he'd have to learn how to cope with surprises on the trail. It was a trade-off."

"A horse trade," Stevie mused as Phil pushed the sliding barn door open. It screeched noisily. "When are you going to get those wheels fixed?" Stevie asked.

"The same day the Marstens get a new pickup truck," Phil said with a grin. The Marstens liked old—if not ramshackle—things. Their pickup truck could be heard blocks away, and their barn, which was a grand old barn with crossed beams on the doors and a Civil War weather vane, had needed a paint job for as long as Stevie had known Phil.

"Ready to meet your mount?" Phil said.

"You bet," she declared eagerly. It was always exciting to meet a new horse, but this horse was especially exciting because Phil had been dropping hints about her all week. This horse, according to Phil, was strong but responsive, brave but canny, spirited but affectionate.

Phil unlatched the stall next to Teddy's and said to Stevie, "Wait out here. I have to get her ready for you."

"Sure," Stevie said, standing back. She knew that it was important to approach a horse the right way. If you got off on the wrong foot with a horse, it could take weeks to get in her good graces—if you ever did.

She could see the horse's dark tail switch back and forth as Phil said something to her. Not that horses can understand English, as Max was always pointing out. Stevie grinned when she realized that Phil was talking to the horse in horse latin. It was Phil's theory that horses may not understand English, but they do understand pig latin, or horse latin.

"Eshay aymay eemsay otay ebay a ittlelay uttynay, utbay eshay siay kayoay," Phil was saying to the horse. Fortunately, or unfortunately, Stevie understood that horse latin was formed by moving the first letter of a word to its end and adding an *ay* so she could tell what Phil was saying—she (Stevie) may be a little nutty, but she is okay.

Stevie crossed her arms. Phil was insulting her to a horse she hadn't even met yet.

"Eshay etsgay a ittlelay catterbrainedsay ometimessay," Phil said, "utbay niay a risiscay eshay ancay eallyray etgay tiay ogethertay."

He could say that again, Stevie thought. She had practically saved his life on the MTO. When Teddy had thrown him and bolted, Stevie had one unconscious rider, Phil, and one scared horse, Topside, to cope with. Luckily, she'd been able to calm Topside, tie him to a tree, and make Phil comfortable. When Max and the other riders arrived, everything was under control.

"Osay ivegay erhay a reakbay," Phil said. "On'tday akemay nyaay napsay udgmentsjay."

That was it! Stevie had heard all she cared to. "Coming in," she called, to warn Phil and the horse that she'd be entering the stall. As she carefully entered, she noticed the horse's tail was switching alertly.

Working her way along the side of the stall, Stevie checked the horse's legs and saw that on her left side she had long white socks—knee socks. And on the other side she had short white socks, anklets. The markings were unusual and very striking. By the time Stevie got to the horse's nose, she was so taken with the beauty of the animal, she forgot to be angry with Phil.

The horse was a light bay mare with an unusually rich brown coat. From her large, intelligent eyes, her small muzzle, and the *mitbah* curve of her head and neck, Stevie could see that she had Arabian blood. But from her rich, thick tail and mane, and her long legs, Stevie could also tell that the horse was part Saddlebred.

"Don't listen to Phil," Stevie said softly, moving slowly around to the front so that she could go eyeball to eyeball with the horse. "He doesn't know a *piaffe* from a *passage*." The *piaffe* and *passage* were the most advanced of all

15

dressage steps. Stevie was excellent at dressage, which was a form of very precise riding.

At this moment the horse pranced in place, doing a step that was very close to the graceful, fluttering motions of a *piaffe*.

"I think she has a sense of humor," Phil said. "And she definitely understands English."

But Stevie was hardly listening. She was looking at the horse's face, which had a long white stripe with a snip above it, so that it looked like an upside-down exclamation point.

"A horse with punctuation," Stevie remarked. "This is unusual. What's her name?"

"She doesn't have a name. We're boarding her for Mr. Baker, who got her in a bulk lot, and her tag said fifty-seven, so we call her Heinz—after Heinz's fifty-seven varieties of sauces," Phil said.

Stevie put her hand under the mare's nose to let her smell it. The horse nuzzled her hand and snorted and then looked directly at Stevie. Those eyes. They were liquid and brown, but with a hint of—

"Yikes," Stevie exclaimed as the horse interrupted Stevie's thoughts by neatly fishing a carrot out of the pocket of her shirt.

"Smart horse," said Phil.

"With a personality like that, you can't call her Heinz," Stevie said. "You might as well call her Miracle Whip."

"I like it," Phil said. "It's much better than Heinz. We'll definitely change her name to Miracle Whip." Stevie turned, about to make a withering remark, when she saw that he was grinning at her.

Stevie tried to think of a name with personality, but she couldn't come up with anything on the spot. "Let's call her No-Name until we can think of something truly great."

"No-Name it is," Phil agreed.

"Mind if I take her outside for a look in the evening light?" Stevie asked. She was dying to watch the Arabian's movements.

"There's no harm in the two of you getting acquainted," Phil said with an extra-casual shrug. Stevie took a closer look at him, because when Phil acted unconcerned like that, there was usually something going on.

Stevie backed No-Name out of the stall and into the corridor and then out into the Marstens' ring. In the twilight the upside-down exclamation point on No-Name's nose gleamed with a pale-blue, almost neon shine, and her white socks flashed in the gathering dusk.

"It looks like she stepped in a bowl of milk," Stevie said.

"I know what you mean," Phil said. "She's so beautiful. But there's something mysterious about her, too."

Stevie ran her hand up No-Name's neck to the end of her mane and then under the mane toward her ears, looking for her special spot. All horses have this spot, the one place they most like to be tickled. No-Name's spot was under her brown forelock, just above the top of the white exclamation point.

As Stevie tickled No-Name, the horse looked as if she were sizing Stevie up. Just like Stewball, Stevie thought warmly.

Whenever The Saddle Club went to visit their friend Kate Devine at The Bar None Dude Ranch out West, Stevie rode a skewbald horse named Stewball. Stewball was smart and independent and Stevie loved riding him. In fact, during the girls' last visit out West, Stevie's parents had given her permission to buy the horse. But then Stevie had realized that Stewball was a ranch horse who needed to be out West, where there was more open space and where he could do what he was good at—being a cattle horse. Cooping him up in a stable would have only made him miserable. Admitting to herself that Stewball was better off at The Bar None, and coming back East without a horse of her own, was one of the hardest things that Stevie had ever done.

Stevie handed the lead to Phil and moved down No-

Name's body, checking her out. No-Name had great legs
—delicate, but strong and long, ideal for dressage.
Healthy hooves. Good rich coat. Except . . .

"Ugh," Stevie said, pulling her hand away from No-
Name's flanks. "Has she been wrestling in mud?"

"Worse," Phil said. "Much worse."

Stevie ran her hand over No-Name's back, sending up
a cloud of dust. "I know. She's been totally neglected."

"That's it, unfortunately," Phil said.

"Let's get a bucket and soap and give her a quick wash.
There's time—and anyway, we can't take her to Cross
County like this," Stevie said. "While we're washing, you
can tell me what happened."

"It's a revolting tale," Phil said.

"I think I have an idea," Stevie said with a grin, because she had three brothers and the word "revolting"
immediately reminded her of them.

As they were searching in the tack room for soap, a
bucket, a towel, and a dandy brush, Stevie said, "So, does
No-Name's condition have anything to do with Rachel?"
Rachel was Phil's ten-year-old sister, who could be pretty
obnoxious at times.

"Why didn't my parents stop while they were ahead?"
Phil groaned as he carried the bucket to the outdoor tap.

Stevie laughed.

"It's not only that No-Name needs to be washed and

groomed," Phil went on. "She has a problem. She's allergic to something. Mr. Baker says that every so often she breaks out in big welts on her head and neck, and no one knows what causes them. It could be fly spray, or saddle soap, or oil on the tack. Or it could be mold in the hay. Judy Barker, our vet, gave us cortisone and antihistamine to reduce the swelling, so we'll just have to see."

"That's tough," Stevie said as she poured a line of water down No-Name's back. "I wouldn't want to have welts all over my face and neck."

"Mr. Baker didn't have time to figure out what she was allergic to, so my dad got this great idea that we could make a trade-off. We'd stable No-Name and get to ride her, and in return Rachel would find out what she was allergic to as a Four-H project."

"I think I know what went wrong." Stevie vigorously brushed No-Name's side. "Rachel."

"Actually, to be fair to Rachel, she had a problem. The minute No-Name arrived here, she stopped getting hives. That made the job of figuring out the cause of the hives much harder. After a few days Rachel decided that she'd raise chickens for her project instead of caring for No-Name."

"I always knew that kid had a screw loose," Stevie said. "Imagine preferring chickens to a horse."

"It's kind of hard to believe," Phil said. "You can't even ride a chicken."

"Maybe Rachel can."

They laughed and stood back to look at No-Name, who wasn't exactly perfectly groomed—they didn't have time—but was now gleaming in the early-evening moonlight. No-Name nickered with pleasure.

"I think she can tell the difference between you and Rachel," Phil said.

"I should hope so!" Stevie said, going with Phil to the tack room to get No-Name's bridle and saddle.

Phil lifted No-Name's bridle from its peg and a saddle from a brace along the wall. "The vet told us that hives can be serious. They start at the muzzle and spread backward, sometimes all the way to the tail. Horses can itch them into sores. They can develop an asthmatic condition, too. And anytime a horse is stressed, he can develop digestive problems, and that means colic."

"Really?" Stevie said. She frowned. That *did* sound serious. Colic could be life threatening.

They walked back outside, and Stevie looked at No-Name's high, intelligent head and brown eyes. She couldn't stand the thought that something might happen to her. From now on, Stevie decided, she would keep a special eye on the beautiful mare. If she could, she would find out what was causing No-Name's terrible hives.

Quickly Stevie tacked up the horse and then mounted her. As she sank gently into the saddle, she sighed with pleasure. This was always one of her favorite moments—feeling herself rise into a different world.

She applied slight pressure with her knees, and No-Name began to walk, tail up, hooves making a brisk clatter on the dirt. No-Name was strong, highly athletic, and seemed to possess a sense of humor, just like Stewball. Somehow, sitting on No-Name's back made Stevie miss Stewball a little less. As she eased herself into an erect, but flexible, riding posture, Stevie thought that No-Name didn't have Stewball's long, loping Western stride. Instead No-Name had a clipped, precise English gait, and this was good. Stevie liked Western riding—it was good for a change of pace—but English was what she had learned first and what would always be her favorite.

Phil was at the gate on Teddy. "Ready?"

"Ready."

Phil bent down, opening the wooden gate. Teddy, who had done this a hundred times, took slow, measured steps while Phil held the gate.

Prancing and sniffing, No-Name walked through the gate. "She needs exercise," Stevie said. "She's been cooped up too long."

"She needs everything," Phil said, "but most of all she needs someone who cares about her."

Stevie could tell that Phil was right. She responded so readily to affection and attention—it was as if she needed a special friend.

"She deserves the best," said Phil.

Stevie glanced over at him. She knew Phil loved horses —all horses, just as she did—but he seemed particularly concerned about No-Name. Stevie had a sudden twinge of curiosity. "You're not planning to sell Teddy and buy No-Name instead?" she asked.

Phil shook his head. "Teddy's the one for me."

As they rode through the hay field behind Phil's house, the horses looked longingly at the long alfalfa stems with purple blossoms. This was the last crop of the year, and the stems of the alfalfa were thick and juicy and the blooms were fat. Winter was coming, and soon the animals would be living on hay. Stevie kept a firm rein on No-Name, letting her know that now was not the right time for feeding. It was bad discipline to let a horse eat with a rider on her back.

When they got to Cross County, the other riders were milling around, getting ready. Riders could be the slowest people on earth, Stevie decided. So she and Phil climbed off their horses and sat on top of the wooden fence, letting the horses graze in the grass and weeds at the bottom of the fence.

"Maybe No-Name is allergic to hay," Stevie commented. Her head was still filled with thoughts about what had caused No-Name's hives.

"That could be," Phil mused. "But she hasn't had an attack since we got her, and she's been eating hay in her stall."

"Hmmm," said Stevie. "It's going to be complicated figuring out what she's allergic to."

"I wouldn't even know where to start," Phil agreed.

At this moment the members of the Cross County Pony Club filed out of the barn.

"At least we'll make it out on the trail before midnight," Stevie muttered to Phil as they got back on their horses.

Mr. Baker lined up the horses, alternating experienced riders with less experienced ones. Phil rode over to the stable manager and said that he and Stevie could bring up the rear.

"That's altruistic of you," Mr. Baker said with a smile. But then he nodded and added, "You and Stevie are experienced riders, just the kind that I need to bring up the end in case anything happens."

When Phil rode back to Stevie, he said, "We're the caboose."

At the other end of the line Mr. Baker lifted his hand and called, "Riders ready?"

"Ready," came voices all down the line. At that Mr. Baker and his horse headed off into the woods.

Stevie, riding just ahead of Phil, called back, "It's a good thing Teddy isn't afraid of the dark anymore." The red harvest moon was low, and shadows were long and wobbly. Twigs and branches seemed to thunder under the horses' hooves.

Next thing Stevie knew, Phil and Teddy were next to her. "I could feel Teddy starting to spook," Phil said. "I guess he's not a hundred percent over it. I think he'll benefit from the companionship of you and No-Name."

"I'm sure," Stevie said, suppressing her grin. Sometimes Phil could be pretty transparent. It wasn't just Teddy he was thinking about; he clearly wanted to be near Stevie. Phil wasn't just a great rider, she thought. He was also a great schemer—almost as good as she was.

The path wound up a hill and through a pine grove, where the ground was silver with needles. Off to the left there was a crash in the underbrush, and a deer came bounding across the path.

Stevie held her breath, because this was exactly what had happened on the MTO—a sudden noise, a deer running across the road, and then Teddy had bucked, throwing Phil. And now, worse yet, it was dark.

Teddy switched his head from side to side, nickering, but held firm.

25

"He'll make it," Phil said, turning toward her in the dark. "You're a good influence. If we'd been alone, I'd still be here, but Teddy would be halfway back to the stable by now."

Next thing Stevie knew, she and Phil were holding hands and riding so close their knees brushed each other. It was a great foursome, Stevie thought, she and Phil and No-Name and Teddy.

As they climbed the hill, the air became cooler and dryer. "We're getting above the river mist," Phil said. At night the Silverado River, which was only a mile away, tended to send off a curl of mist that lay low over the fields and then rolled up the ravines.

"Mr. Weatherman," Stevie teased.

"Hey," Phil said, "I'm just looking ahead. You never know."

Suddenly there was a ripple of excitement down the line of horses. When it reached No-Name, she switched her tail. Teddy tossed his head, as if he were agreeing with her. Stevie looked up and saw that the clouds seemed closer now. They were so low and flat and bright that she felt as if she could touch them.

"Ideal conditions," Phil said, looking up at the clouds.

Ideal for what? Stevie wondered. But before she could ask him, there was a clearing ahead, and the horses broke into an easy trot. Rising in her seat, feeling No-Name's

26

excitement, Stevie looked ahead and saw a field of hay in the moonlight. In sunlight, she knew, this field would be dusted with pink and purple flowers, but now, in the moonlight, it seemed ⌄o be made of silver.

Mr. Baker's voice floated back from the front, telling them they were going to canter and that they should stay on the trail—the farmer who owned this land wouldn't appreciate their going into his field. As Mr. Baker gave a signal, Stevie touched No-Name's belly behind her girth, giving her permission to canter.

No-Name took off, head stretching forward, ears up, loving it, ready to run forever. Stevie had a flash of some Arabian ancestor of No-Name's galloping along a desert track, fierce and indefatigable, running toward the desert moon.

Teddy and Phil were beside them, matching them step for step. Stevie looked over and saw Phil's green eyes widen as he looked over the hill ahead. Stevie looked ahead and saw that a finger of mist had crept up a ravine onto this part of the hill.

"Riders, slow," came Mr. Baker's voice.

Stevie put her hand on No-Name's neck and leaned back, wondering if No-Name would respond. A tremor ran along No-Name's neck because, as Stevie knew, she had just been getting warmed up. But No-Name slowed to a walk. A few minutes later, they were enveloped by the mist. Stevie could barely make out the other riders and horses.

Next to her Phil reached for her hand. As he leaned over in his saddle to kiss her, she bent toward him, but their romantic moment was interrupted by No-Name, who whinnied and pranced. Next thing Stevie knew, she and Phil were hanging on to each other to keep from falling off their horses. With a tremendous effort Stevie pulled herself back into her saddle. Phil did the same.

"Riders assemble." Mr. Baker's voice floated through the mist.

As Stevie and Phil rode out of the fog, Mr. Baker loomed up in front of them in his black riding helmet and tweed hacking jacket. "Mist is rising from the valley," he said. "It can make footing treacherous and uncertain. We'll have to head back for the stable."

There was a discontented murmuring among the riders, but everyone knew that Mr. Baker was right.

"Phil and Stevie, you lead the way back," Mr. Baker said.

With twelve riders behind them, staring at their backs, the chances for a kiss did not look good, Stevie thought. She smiled to herself, thinking about No-Name's reaction to her leaning out of the saddle, and she leaned forward to pat No-Name's neck affectionately. But No-Name twitched to throw off Stevie's hand. Thanks a lot, Stevie thought. First you wreck a kiss and now you won't let me pat you. I thought we were friends.

Then Stevie realized that No-Name's coat felt unaccountably lumpy. She peered at the horse more closely, straining to see in the moonlight.

It couldn't be. But it was. There was a lump on the tender curve of No-Name's left ear. Another at its base. As Stevie frantically examined the area around No-Name's head and neck, she felt welts on No-Name's muzzle and the underside of her neck.

No-Name had hives.

"She's allergic to the soap we used," Stevie whispered in horror. "No, she's probably allergic to *me*."

3

"IT WASN'T AS much fun as I thought it would be," Stevie admitted.

"What could be bad about a moonlight ride?" asked Carole as she chewed on the end of a straw. The three members of The Saddle Club were holding a brief Saddle Club meeting before class on Tuesday afternoon.

"It started off fine," Stevie told them. "I was riding this great horse that's staying at Phil's stable."

"What's the horse's name?" Lisa asked.

"No-Name," Stevie said.

"A horse has got to have a name," Carole said, crossing her arms.

"She does," Stevie said. "Her name is No-Name."

Carole and Lisa rolled their eyes, both of them thinking that this was the Steviest of all possible names.

"So anyway," Stevie said, "here Phil and I were on this romantic ride, and not only did we have moonlight, we had mist."

"Very handy," Lisa said with a smile.

"We were totally alone and we were about to have . . ."

"The kiss of the century?" Carole said.

"That's it," Stevie said. "But No-Name started dancing in place."

"Doing a *piaffe?*" Carole said.

Stevie frowned, thinking about Carole's question. Now that she thought about it, No-Name *had* been doing the *piaffe* in the middle of the mist. Once again Stevie wondered about No-Name. Obviously she'd had some training in dressage; so how had she wound up in the bulk lot of horses that Mr. Baker had acquired?

"I've got to meet this horse," Carole said. "She sounds special."

"She is," Stevie agreed eagerly. "She has white socks on all of her legs, and this really unusual upside-down exclamation point on her face. . . ." She went on and on, telling her friends every detail about the beautiful Arabian.

A red car pulled up in the Pine Hollow driveway, and

31

Hollie Bright jumped out and ran halfway to the barn. Then, as if it was an afterthought, she turned and waved to her mother, who was at the wheel of the car. Her mother gestured and said something, which caused Hollie to give a large, exaggerated shrug, shoulders up, hands out, as if to say—how can parents be so silly?

Lisa smiled, remembering how her own mother had hovered the first time she rode at Pine Hollow, simultaneously assuring Max that Lisa was a fantastic rider and trying to make sure she wouldn't fall off and get killed.

"I'm glad you're early," Lisa said to Hollie.

"Me too," said Stevie.

"Me three," said Carole.

"The whole Saddle Club is here," Hollie said. "This is an honor."

"We want to get you off to a good start," said Lisa, remembering her first day again, when she'd thought that Stevie was a creep and Veronica diAngelo, the stable brat, was an angel. Lisa had definitely gotten off on the wrong foot. She didn't want the same thing to happen to Hollie.

"Come and meet Delilah, the horse you're going to ride," Carole said. "You'll love her."

As they walked toward the entrance to the stable, Stevie pointed to the horseshoe nailed to the wall over the outside mounting block. "If you want to make sure that nothing goes wrong, remember to touch the horse-shoe before you head out on the trail. Because of it, nothing really serious has ever gone wrong at Pine Hollow."

"That's because it reminds riders to be careful," Carole said earnestly. "Not because it's magic."

"We could have used a horseshoe backstage at *Annie*," Hollie said to Lisa. "Especially on opening night when everyone was afraid they were going to forget their lines."

"I could have used one Sunday night," Stevie said with a sigh. "Talk about things going wrong."

Carole and Lisa looked at her. "So far your ride sounds wonderful," Lisa said. "What went wrong?"

Stevie briefly filled Hollie in about her ride on No-Name. Then she continued with her sad tale. "On the way home No-Name came down with hives. Her face and neck were covered with them. And it's all because Phil and I washed her."

"Back up," Carole said. "What did you wash her with?"

"Horse soap."

Carole shook her head. "Horse soap is usually hypoallergenic, which means that it doesn't give horses hives." This was something that she knew from her work with Judy Barker.

"That's a relief," Stevie said. "I felt like I should be put in horse prison."

Hollie shrugged. "I have allergies from time to time,

33

and it's no big deal. I just ignore them." She turned to Stevie. "The hives probably bothered you more than they did the horse."

"Actually," Stevie said, "No-Name seemed remarkably calm."

"Hives don't harm a horse," Carole said, "unless the horse scratches them until they're sore."

"Another danger is that the horse will get so upset, it develops digestive troubles," Carole said.

"Right," Stevie said. She knew that emotions frequently affected a horse's stomach.

"A horse with stomach trouble can develop diarrhea or colic," Carole said. "And if colic isn't treated, it can result in death."

"Great." Stevie shook her head. "I was worried before, but now I'm terrified."

They had reached Delilah's stall. Delilah, the gentlest and easiest to ride of all the Pine Hollow horses, had her nose in her hay bag.

"Come on," Carole said, taking Hollie by the arm. "I'll introduce you. You're really going to like Delilah, and she's going to like you."

Fifteen minutes later Hollie led Delilah into the outdoor ring, touching the good-luck horseshoe on her way. She got up on the block and mounted, looking eager and excited.

Lisa kept a close eye on her friend, wanting to be as helpful to her as Hollie had been to Lisa at the beginning of rehearsals.

Obviously, Hollie's earlier riding lessons had stayed with her. She kept her hands low, her heels down, knees tucked in, and back straight. Most important, she was in communication with her horse, checking Delilah to make sure that she was alert and attentive. Pretty soon the two of them looked as if they'd been together forever. Seeing this, Lisa relaxed. She was more glad than ever she'd invited Hollie to Pine Hollow.

As part of the class, Max had Carole demonstrate some "wrong" ways of jumping. One of these was "calling a cab," when a rider held up her hand as if trying to hail a taxi. As all the riders could see, this threw Starlight off balance, making her clip the rail with her right rear hoof. Then Carole demonstrated another common error, the "suicide tilt," leaning too far back in the saddle. At first the jump looked great because there was so little weight over Starlight's front legs, but then the extra weight on her hindquarters prevented her hind legs from rising, so they knocked the top rail from the fence.

Then, to show how jumping ought to be done, Carole and Starlight trotted along the edge of the ring with Carole leaning low over Starlight's neck. Carole seemed totally relaxed as Starlight moved smoothly toward the jump. Horse and rider rose into the air and sailed over the fence. Then they came down in a perfect landing.

"See how easy it is," Max said, his eyes bright with pleasure. "You just have to let your horse jump."

Next to Lisa, Hollie muttered, "That's like saying anyone can play Hamlet."

Lisa giggled. "You have a point. But Max is a great teacher. I wouldn't have made as much progress as I have if it weren't for him."

Hollie looked uncertain. "We'll see how I do."

But by the time Hollie had completed the first exercise, Lisa was more than a little impressed.

"I was watching you," she called to her friend. "That was almost perfect form. I think you're a natural because of all your acting experience."

"You mean you dink it's because I'm faking riding?" Hollie said, and let loose with a sneeze.

Lisa shook her head. "It's because you have self-confidence. You don't get tense and self-conscious. Delilah's pretty cool, but even she gets nervous with a beginner on her back."

"Do you dink you could give me a dissue?" Hollie said.

Lisa blinked, trying to figure out what Hollie had said. Then she realized that Hollie was asking for a tissue. "Sure," Lisa said, searching in an inside pocket in her riding jacket. This proved that Hollie knew her really well, Lisa thought. Because all of Lisa's jackets and coats had packets of tissues put there by Lisa's mother. "Help yourself," she said, passing Hollie a new pack. "Do you have a cold?"

Hollie shook her head. "Danks, I'm edernally dateful."

Lisa opened her mouth, about to tell Hollie that she was "endirely delcome," when she noticed Max looking at them with irritation. With her eyes, Lisa signaled to Hollie that there was trouble, and Hollie blew her nose as softly as possible and slipped the tissues into the pocket of her riding jacket.

After class Lisa explained that Max didn't like people to talk for any reason when they were at a class or at a meeting of the Pony Club. "He says concentration is the most important part of riding," she said.

"He sounds like my acting doach," said Hollie with a sound that was halfway between a laugh and a sneeze.

"Hey," Lisa said, rising from her saddle, "there's Judy Barker. She's the vet here at Pine Hollow." She pointed to a woman in jeans climbing out of a blue pickup truck. "If you think Carole knows a lot about horses," she went on, "Judy knows more. In fact," she added with a grin, "Carole's ambition is to grow up to be Judy."

"Maybe," Carole chimed in. "I'm still not sure if I want to be a trainer or a breeder or a vet."

37

"Whatever it is, it'll involve horses—right?" Hollie asked.

"How'd you guess?" Stevie put in. The four girls laughed.

Later, when Judy got to Topside's stall, Stevie bombarded her with questions. "How do you find out what a horse is allergic to? Can you treat allergies easily? What if the horse—"

"Whoa," Judy said, looking up from the shot that she was about to give Topside. "Who's allergic?"

"A horse at the Marstens'," Stevie said.

Judy finished giving Topside the shot and then massaged the spot to ease the sting and get the serum circulating. "You mean the horse they're boarding?" Judy said. When Stevie nodded, Judy said, "I saw the horse just after they got her. They wanted me to check her bone splint, which is just fine, and her allergies. I couldn't tell right off about the allergies, though I can do some tests. Allergies in horses are a lot like allergies in humans— they're hard to track down. Have you ever had a friend with allergies?"

Stevie shook her head and said, "No." But then she remembered that Hollie had said something about having an allergy, so she said, "Actually, yes."

"Your friend can tell you that almost anything can cause an allergy. It's the same with animals. It could be the horse's food, or weeds in the pasture, or bug spray, or saddle soap," Judy said. "Or it could be a combination of all of them."

"Great," Stevie said. "Is No-Name going to go around for the rest of her life covered with welts?"

"That's the name of the horse?" asked Judy with a smile.

"For the time being," Stevie said. "Until I think of a permanent one."

Judy put the empty syringe in a pocket on the side of her bag. "You can usually treat hives with cortisone and antihistamine. The Marstens called me last night, and I told them to use the antihistamine." She smiled at Stevie. "You'll be glad to know that No-Name was fine in half an hour."

"But what if it gets worse?" Stevie said. "Can't a horse get more and more allergic?"

Judy looked at Stevie, her expression serious. "That can happen. That's why we watch allergies so closely—and why we try to get to the bottom of them. It's also why stables have to be ready for allergy emergencies—in both horses and humans. You know the first-aid box in the tack room?"

Stevie nodded. The red, white, and blue first-aid box stuck out like a sore thumb among the brown saddles and tack.

"There's an EpiPen inside for any human who has an allergic reaction to a bee sting, or anything else," Judy explained. "When that happens, the person's air passages swell so badly that they can't breathe. The medicine reduces the swelling and keeps them from suffocating. And for horses Mrs. Reg has cortisone and antihistamine on hand. An injection takes half an hour, the powder a little longer. Plus, you can always call me," Judy said with a smile, putting her hand on Stevie's arm. "Allergies aren't usually dangerous unless you ignore them."

"I'm going to hunt down the cause of No-Name's allergy if it's the last thing I do," Stevie said to Judy.

"Good for you," Judy said. "It's going to take luck and patience."

"Hmmm," Stevie said. "Luck is fun; patience I'm not so sure about."

"NO-NAME WAS BETTER in half an hour," Phil said that
night over the phone.

"I guess you must have given her a shot rather than a
powder," Stevie said.

"How did you know?" asked Phil, sounding startled.

"My deep knowledge of horse medicine, plus a conver-
sation with Judy Barker."

"She's been treating No-Name, but it's frustrating because we can't find out anything about her past," Phil
said. "No one knows her previous history, so we don't
know what kind of fly spray her previous owners used, or
soap, or anything."

"It probably wasn't the soap," said Stevie, showing off

her new knowledge, "because most soaps are hypoallergenic."

"Hypo what?" Phil said.

" 'Hypo' is the opposite of 'hyper,' " said Stevie, who had looked it up in the dictionary. " 'Hypoallergenic' means 'low allergy.' "

"You're a human dictionary," Phil said.

But meanwhile Stevie was thinking that it was time for the allergy detective, namely her, to go into high gear. For a second Stevie imagined herself in a Sherlock Holmes cap with a huge magnifying glass examining No-Name's food and bedding.

"How would you like to spend more time around No-Name?" Phil said.

"Would I!" Stevie said. "In fact you can't keep me away. I'm going to find out what No-Name's allergic to."

"I could tell you liked her," Phil said.

"I'm crazy about her," Stevie said. "She has personality. She has character. She has a certain . . ."

"Stevie-ness?" Phil said.

"You might put it that way," Stevie acknowledged.

"Come over to my place on Friday," Phil said. "We can go riding and to the movies."

"Great," Stevie said. She could picture the evening already. They'd ride, then discuss Teddy and No-Name through dinner, then choose a movie with horses in it.

Mr. Marsten would probably drive them to the movie in the family pickup truck, which always had odds and ends of horse gear in the back. For a horse-crazy girl, it was the best possible kind of date.

"I can't wait," she added.

"One other thing," Phil said casually.

She knew Phil's 'other' things. They were usually the main thing, so she said, "Yeeeeeees?"

"Cross County is going to be taking part in a dressage exhibition," Phil said. "And nobody's better at dressage than you."

"I'm not so sure about that," Stevie said modestly.

"Don't tell me you've got some competition from another member of Horse Wise," Phil said.

"Carole and Starlight are getting pretty good," she replied.

"They're still not as tight and disciplined as you," Phil remarked. "Mr. Baker has given me a dressage test to practice, and I was hoping you could give me some pointers. Teddy is a good horse for dressage—he has those strong hindquarters, and he's smart and takes direction well. The problem is me. I always make it look like work."

"That's bad," Stevie said. The heart of dressage was making it look as if the horse were doing everything from his own free will. The constant signals from the rider needed to be invisible.

"I'm like a magician who telegraphs his tricks," Phil said. "When it comes time to change tacks, you can see me sawing away with the reins. I get Teddy so agitated, he practically tips over."

"Whoa!" Stevie said. "The first rule in dressage is to respect your horse's judgment and not try to do everything yourself."

"I can see that I have a lot to learn from you."

"It's taken you this long to figure that out?" Stevie teased.

"So you'll teach me?" Phil said. "It's a trade?"

"I can ride No-Name as much as I want in return for helping you with your dressage?" said Stevie dreamily. "Mmmmm. I think you've got yourself a deal."

"So I'll see you on Friday," Phil said.

"I think I've almost got my parents persuaded to let me take the commuter bus to Berryville," Stevie said. Berryville was a tiny town within walking distance of the Marstens' place. "Tonight I'll really work on them, and by Friday—with a little luck—I'll be riding that bus." Until now, whenever Stevie wanted to go over to Phil's, she'd had to get one of her parents to drive her. Since both her parents were lawyers who worked in Washington, D.C., this was no easy matter.

Stevie said good night to Phil, then hung up the phone

and raced quickly downstairs. It was never too soon to get started working on her parents.

The next day, which was Wednesday, The Saddle Club planned to meet at Pine Hollow after school. They had so much to talk about that it seemed to Stevie that Wednesday was the longest school day in human history. Usually she liked math, kind of, but today the fifty minutes felt like fifty hours. Did her English teacher really have to read so much of A Midsummer Night's Dream out loud? And did the Fenton Hall cafeteria have to have a four-block line that ended with mystery lasagna?

By the time Stevie got to Pine Hollow to meet Lisa and Carole, she was frazzled. But once she had checked Topside's water and put some fresh hay in the hay bag, and checked the straw underfoot and found that it was still dry and clean, she began to feel calmer.

She wandered into the tack room and stared at the bridles and halters hanging from pegs and at the coils of straps on the floor. Usually, she wasn't crazy about cleaning tack, but now the leathery smell and faint dustiness of the tack room seemed cozy and welcoming.

Looking at the black velvet riding helmets that hung on the wall above the tack, she got a sudden idea. For some reason the fact that No-Name had no name was bothering her. It was one of the reasons that she'd had trouble concentrating today. No-Name seemed to have no medical history and no past, almost as if she didn't exist.

Stevie reached up and took down some of the hats. Then she rearranged them on the wall to spell "No-Name."

"What's this? A protest of some kind?" said Lisa from behind Stevie. From the straw on Lisa's boots, Stevie could tell she'd been mucking out Prancer's stall.

"Kind of," Stevie said, flopping down on a pile of horse blankets. "It's a protest against No-Name's lack of a name."

"I can see that," Lisa said. She sat down next to Stevie and stretched out her legs. "Don't you know *anything* about her?"

Stevie shook her head. "Only that she belongs to Mr. Baker, who got her from a bulk lot."

"Hi, guys." Carole came through the doorway with a thick horse manual under her arm. "What's new?"

"Stevie's in love," Lisa said.

"I knew that," Carole said with a twinkle in her eye.

"Not with Phil," Lisa said. "With No-Name."

"She's right," Stevie agreed. "Luckily I'll be seeing a lot of her in the coming weeks. I'm going to be over at Phil's helping him with his dressage for an exhibition. And I'll also be figuring out what makes No-Name allergic."

"Great," Carole groaned. "I don't mean to be selfish or

anything. But first Lisa was off working on *Annie*; now you'll be over at Phil's. When is The Saddle Club ever going to be together again? We're practically not a club anymore."

"The dressage exhibition is only a couple of weeks away," Stevie said. "And I won't be there all the time. Anyway, I'm worried about No-Name. This horse is practically an orphan."

"Dressage?" came a voice from the doorway. They all jumped and saw Max, his blue eyes gleaming. "This reminds me that Horse Wise has been invited to a certain dressage exhibition in almost two weeks," he said.

"Could it be?" Stevie said.

Max smiled. He'd met Phil several times, and he knew that not only was Phil a member of Cross County, but also that he and Stevie liked each other.

"You've got it, Stevie," Max said. "The exhibition is at Cross County. Mr. Baker is an excellent riding instructor and horse trainer, so I'm sure we'll have a lot to learn."

Stevie was elated that the members of The Saddle Club, as well as the rest of Horse Wise, would be at the dressage exhibition. She resolved to work as hard as she could with Phil so that he'd knock them out with his dressage skills.

* * *

47

When Phil met Stevie at the commuter bus stop on Friday, he stared at her in disbelief, as if she were an illusion of some kind. "I can't believe your parents actually let you take the bus."

"I wasn't sure they were going to until this morning," Stevie answered. "We were still discussing it at breakfast."

"No-Name is eager to see you," Phil said. "No more welts, no more symptoms."

"I missed her," Stevie said. "I've been thinking about her all week."

Phil kicked a rock and grinned. "I was thinking that if you were a horse, you'd probably have an upside-down exclamation point on your nose, too."

"Thanks a lot," Stevie said, but she didn't entirely mind the idea.

The Marstens' house was one of the oldest in the area, built of irregular gray stones that seemed to have grown into each other. The chimney was made of bricks so old that their corners had worn off. The house wasn't fancy— that wasn't the Marstens' style; instead it had simply become a beautiful part of the landscape.

At an upper window Stevie saw a grinning face topped by soft brown curls.

"Great," Phil said, looking up. "I thought Rachel had karate class this afternoon."

"She's into karate?"

"Karate and chickens," Phil said. "Though why she needs karate, I don't know. It can't be self-defense. People run when they see her."

Rachel appeared in the doorway of the Marsten house and said, "Hi, Stevie, coming to see your booooooooooooyfriend?"

Stevie smirked. This was just the kind of feeble thing her younger brother Michael would say. She shrugged and said, "That's about it, Rach."

Clearly, this wasn't the response that Rachel had expected. She looked at Phil and said, "I guess she fell for it, Phil. You must think you're pretty clever."

"Come on, Stevie," Phil said, turning toward the barn.

Alarms went off in Stevie's head. She didn't want anyone to think she was a fool, not even a ten-year-old. "Fell for what?" she said to Rachel.

"The horse thing," said Rachel, putting her hands on her hips. "He knew you would," she added.

"What horse thing?" Stevie said, turning to Phil.

But it was Rachel who answered. "He wanted this silly horse to stay here, so he kept telling everyone that I was going to find out what she was allergic to. Like I'm really going to do that. I don't even like horses."

The wheels in Stevie's mind whirred. Rachel had never really offered to find out what No-Name was allergic to? The whole thing had been an invention by Phil so that

49

No-Name could stay, and Stevie would visit his place more often?

Stevie turned to Phil and saw that his face was beet-red. Phil was blushing! How sweet, Stevie thought. However, it was also embarrassing for Phil, and she didn't want to make him feel totally humiliated. She turned to Rachel and said, "Too bad you have such an empty life."

"What do you mean?" Rachel said, looking indignant.

"Following your brother around all the time. Neglecting your life to poke into his. It's kind of sad, really. Ask your teacher to see if you can get a pen pal or something. Lonely kids like you often get a lot of benefit from friends in far-off places."

That did it. Rachel was gone.

"Thanks," Phil said, looking at the empty doorway where Rachel had been. "I get so angry at her that I want to clobber her. But if I clobber her, my parents won't like it."

"Parents tend to frown on clobbering," said Stevie, remembering a couple of bad experiences of her own.

"Next time I'll try using humor," Phil said, though he didn't sound hopeful about it.

"It's easier to be funny with someone else's brother or sister," Stevie said. "With Michael I always go right over the edge."

"So you know what it's like," said Phil.

"Those are among my worst memories," Stevie assured him. "But don't worry, we'll get back at Rachel. In a nice way, of course."

"Nice, but not too nice," Phil said. "Let's not go overboard with the niceness."

"Okay," Stevie agreed. As they headed toward the stable, Stevie's thoughts turned back to her plan to unmask the substance that was causing No-Name's allergy. Likely candidates were the fly spray used before rides to keep No-Name's eyes clear, saddle soap from a newly cleaned saddle, and No-Name's regular snacks, which were carrots and apples. Of course she couldn't eliminate all these things from No-Name's life—it wouldn't be fair to deprive her of apples and carrots, and if she was never sprayed again, flies would drive her crazy. What Stevie was going to do was use a technique that Judy Barker had suggested. Each day for three days she'd use one possible allergy causer on No-Name. The first time it would be fly spray, the next it would be saddle soap, and the next it would be snack food. Today Stevie decided to test fly spray. So she sprayed No-Name's head liberally.

When she and No-Name met Phil and Teddy in the Marstens' outdoor ring a few minutes later, Phil sniffed the air. "Phew. What's that smell?"

Stevie felt a little embarrassed. "Fly spray. I'm checking

to see if No-Name is allergic to any of the ingredients in this brand."

"If she is, we'll know soon," Phil said, moving Teddy to the side to get out of smelling range. "Ready for the dressage lesson?"

"Ready," Stevie said. "So which is Teddy's stiff side?"

"His left," Phil replied. Stevie knew that the muscles on a horse's stiff side were longer than they were on his soft side. This was because horses naturally favored one side over the other, just the way humans favor their right or left hand.

"Can I see?" Stevie asked, backing No-Name into the center of the ring so she could watch.

Phil urged Teddy into a sitting trot, a gait that was gentle enough so that he didn't have to post. Teddy was now turning toward his left, his stiff side, and stretching his right side, his soft side. A horse who hadn't been trained would resist this maneuver. But Teddy was trotting easily, and Stevie could see that Phil was using a minimum of rein contact.

"You've been working with him," she commented.

"Hey, Teddy deserves the best," Phil said with a happy smile.

"How about some figure eights?" Stevie said.

"With pleasure," Phil said, turning toward the center of the ring. When Teddy got to the middle of the eight and

moved to the left, Stevie saw how supple his spine was—
this was also the result of good training, she knew. Stevie
also saw that Teddy changed his bend from left to right
with no resistance.

"That's good," Stevie said, truly encouraged. Phil had
said that he needed a lot of help, but he was clearly off to
a good start. He and Teddy should do fine at dressage.

"How about a turn on the forehand?" Stevie called out.

Keeping his front feet in one spot and using them as a
pivot, Teddy moved his hindquarters in a circle. To do
this, Teddy's hind legs had to step across each other, a
thing that most horses truly hated. Again Teddy showed
no sign of nervousness or reluctance. This was a well-
trained horse.

"And now for the ultimate toughie, the countercanter," Stevie said.

"I don't know," Phil said. "We've worked on it,
but . . ." His voice trailed off. He put his hand on
Teddy's neck and said something that Stevie couldn't
hear. He and Teddy cantered clockwise around the ring;
then he brought Teddy off the rail and started him cantering in the opposite direction without changing leads.

Stevie's jaw dropped. The countercanter was a movement that a lot of riders wouldn't even try. It was
extremely difficult to get an untrained horse to countercanter, because an untrained horse wants to be on the left

lead when he's cantering left. Actually, that's not even what an untrained horse wants to do, it's what he has to do because he's not supple enough to go on an opposite lead. But here was Teddy cantering left on a right lead. And now Teddy was moving away from the rail and then back into it in a serpentine pattern without changing leads.

"I can't believe it," Stevie said as a smiling Phil rode up to her. "Have you guys been practicing day and night?"

"Teddy wanted to impress you," Phil said with a grin. "I told him he was overreaching himself, but you know how Teddy is."

Stevie was totally thunderstruck by this display. Phil had always been a good rider with great natural instincts, and Teddy had always been a fine horse, but now they had passed to a new level. Taking a close look at Teddy, she could see that he had become better balanced, more muscular, and above all more self-confident.

"There's only one thing," Stevie said. "You don't need my help. You two are great."

Phil's face fell. Was working together on dressage another part of Phil's plan to spend more time with Stevie?

There must be a solution to this, Stevie thought. "So you'll do something else." She searched around wildly for an idea. "Something beyond dressage."

"Like what?" Phil said gloomily. "There isn't anything beyond dressage."

Suddenly, she didn't know why, Stevie saw Lisa at the end of *Annie*, stepping down to the edge of the stage and singing "Tomorrow." She could hear Lisa's husky voice and feel the hush of the crowd.

"With music," she said, still thinking. "You'll ride to music."

"Teddy loves heavy-metal rock," Phil joked.

Stevie giggled. "I don't know about heavy metal. But we'll think of something."

"You'll join me, Stevie? There's no way I can do this alone," Phil said.

"A duet," Stevie said. "I'm into it."

Actually, she couldn't wait to get started working with Phil on a dressage duet. Not only would it be fun to spend time with him, she'd have a chance to find out how much dressage training No-Name had had in her past.

So what if Stevie didn't have a clue about how to create a horse duet? Her friends in The Saddle Club would help her and Phil figure out a horse-dancing routine.

"FIRST, IT IS essential that a horse be active and free but still display its inherent strength and speed."

Hollie rolled her eyes, looking at Lisa as if to ask what they were doing there. It was a Saturday morning at Pine Hollow Stables, and the wind from the Silverado Mountains was fresh, the flowers in the pasture on the other side of the fence sparkling with dew. So what were they doing listening to this dull woman drone on about dressage?

Lisa rolled her eyes, too, to show that she agreed the speaker was boring—she didn't want Hollie to think she thought that everything that had to do with horses was exciting. She had her limits, too. But then Lisa looked back to the speaker because she knew that if she didn't pay attention, Max would blast her afterward. Max hated talking during Horse Wise meetings, but he hated talking even more when they had a guest speaker. Lisa shifted to her other foot and turned her attention back to the speaker.

"Horses are athletes," the woman was saying in a nasal voice, "and so are riders. Dressage is a way of getting horse and rider in shape."

This made sense, Lisa thought, but for a new rider like Hollie, the only way to really understand dressage was to experience it. The first time Hollie got her horse to lengthen his stride without quickening it, the first time she experienced that odd floating feeling, she'd understand why some people, like Stevie, loved dressage. That floating sensation was what a ballerina feels at the top of her leap, or a basketball player feels at the moment of a slam dunk. For a moment you're not earthbound. You are one with your horse.

"To be a dressage judge requires accuracy of mind, a deep knowledge of horse anatomy, and courage," the speaker said.

Lisa heard a muffled squeak and looked over to Hollie. Her friend was in severe danger of breaking out in giggles. The speaker had made a dressage judge sound like Superman. It's a bird, it's a plane, no, it's a dressage judge, Lisa thought. She grinned herself and then smothered the grin because she could feel Max's eyes on her.

"At the exhibition at Cross County you will be able to see dressage judging at its finest," said the speaker with a satisfied smile. "No actual prizes will be awarded, but the judge, namely myself, will offer insightful comments."

"It'll be standing room only," Hollie muttered.

Lisa gave her a warning look, but it was too late. Max walked to the center of the ring and said, "I hope you've all been listening." He looked directly at Hollie. "Because now we're going to put the principles of dressage in action."

Hollie sighed, and Lisa could tell that she was wishing she were somewhere else.

When all the riders were mounted, Max nodded toward Hollie's horse. "Some horses, like Delilah, have a tendency to let their heads droop. Does anyone know how to get a horse to raise its head?"

"You pull on the reins," said Hollie, and she pulled Delilah's reins without waiting for Max to answer. Delilah's head went up, but now it was too high, giving her a stiff, uncomfortable look.

"That's how you *don't* do it," Max said sharply. He never liked to see a horse in discomfort.

"Sorry," Hollie said, loosening the reins and slumping.

"Who knows?" Max said.

No one raised her hand, because no one wanted to make Hollie look bad.

"It's not your fault," Max said, turning back to Hollie, "but next time find out what to do before doing it. It's not fair to experiment on your horse." He looked back at the group. "Anyone know?"

Carole raised her hand. "You have to get her back legs farther under her. Delilah tends to walk with her hind legs sticking out. If you get them under her haunches, her head will go up."

"Right," Max said.

Lisa, who was proud of how well Carole had explained Delilah's droopy-head problem, looked at Hollie to see if she was impressed. But to Lisa's disappointment Hollie was staring at the road that ran to Pine Hollow. Clearly, Hollie was wishing she were someplace else. Lisa felt terrible because Hollie wasn't finding Pine Hollow as much fun as she'd expected.

After class, when the horses had been unsaddled and groomed, The Saddle Club met in the tack room. Hollie was already there, sitting on a pile of horse blankets, looking glumly at the tangles of tack on the opposite wall.

"I don't know if horseback riding is for me," she said to Lisa. "No applause. No makeup. No audience. I think maybe I'm too much of a lightweight to be a serious rider."

"Hey," Lisa said, flopping down next to her. "Were you a star after your first acting lesson?"

"No." Hollie had a wry expression. "I'm certainly not a star now either."

"It's not so different from learning to act," Lisa insisted. "You have to master technique, study the greats, and tune your instrument."

"I didn't know you played an instrument," Stevie said, popping open a soda can.

"An actor's body is her instrument," Lisa said. "She has to keep it fit and well tuned."

"Same thing with dressage," Stevie said, and took a sip of her soda. "Horses are basically kind of stiff and bulky. Dressage makes them supple and graceful."

"It's like a strengthen-and-stretch class," Lisa said. "Plus it's like aerobics. Plus it's like a total body workout."

"And a total mind workout," Carole said. "The heart of dressage is rider-horse communication. It has to be based on a set of shared signals, which can be anything from the pressure of a knee to a slight change in the balance of the rider."

Lisa could see that Carole was getting overly serious and that Hollie was losing interest again.

"It's like dancing," Stevie said suddenly. "That's what it's really like. When things are going right, you and the horse don't even have to communicate with each other—you just know."

"I know what you mean," Hollie said, sitting up straight. "When you're performing, you have to forget about everything you've learned and dance the music. You have to dance it like you're hearing it for the first time, as if you don't know what note comes next."

"That's it!" As Stevie jumped up, her soda sloshed on her knee, making a dark spot on her breeches. "I was telling Phil that we needed to add something extra to the dressage exhibition, something with music." She looked at Hollie excitedly. "You could help us. You could be our choreographer."

"Me?" Hollie said, looking somewhat stunned at this new idea.

"You helped with the dance numbers in *Annie*," Stevie said. "You told Lisa that blocking them out was your favorite part."

"Horses can't dance," Hollie said, crossing her arms. "I know they're wonderful and fascinating and stuff, but they can't exactly dance."

"That's what you think," said Stevie.

Carole and Lisa sat grinning at Stevie. Now Lisa shook her head. "You and Phil are going to dance with your horses in Cross County's exhibition?"

Stevie flushed. "It sounds a little silly, but I thought it would be fun."

"I think it's a great idea," Carole chimed in. "Very Stevian."

"Thanks, Carole," Stevie remarked.

"What makes you think it was a compliment?" Carole teased her. Then she glanced suddenly at her watch. "Whoops. I'd better go. I promised my dad I'd go to something at the base." Carole's father was a colonel in the Marine Corps, stationed at Quantico, and sometimes Carole went with him to functions at the base. Carole's mother had died a few years ago, and she and her father were very close.

"I have to go, too," Lisa said, standing up. "I have this paper due in three weeks and I haven't even started the research."

"Three weeks!" Stevie said. "Are you bonkers? It's too soon to even think about the paper."

But Lisa was heading for the door.

"I guess it's just you and me," Stevie said to Hollie with a grin. "So are you up to being our choreographer?"

"Sure," Hollie answered.

"Okay, stand up." When Hollie looked surprised, Stevie explained that they might as well be comfortable. She dragged the pile of horse blankets into a corner, where she rolled up two and propped them against the wall as backrests. Then she went into Mrs. Reg's office next door and borrowed a sheet of paper and a pencil.

"Okay," she said, flopping down next to Hollie, "how do we go about this?"

Hollie leaned back and closed her eyes. "The main thing is that you have to have a deam," she said.

"Sure," Stevie said. "I knew that. How do you spell 'deam'?"

"What?" Hollie said, looking surprised.

"Deam. Is it 'deem' with two *e*'s?"

"Not deam . . . deam," Hollie said.

Stevie was beginning to feel totally confused.

Hollie sneezed loudly, then said, "I mean 'deam.'" She spelled it out. "T-H-E-M-E."

"Oh, *theme*," Stevie said, writing it down. "Good idea. What could it be?"

Hollie sniffed and said, "You look at what your deatrical assets are."

"Hunh?" Stevie said.

"What's best about the dancers, horses, whatever. And you play on that," Hollie said. "Like the dicest thing about you and Phil is that you're a douple."

"Couple?" Stevie asked.

"That's it," Hollie said. "You really like each other.

63

And this will show up in your dancing. Do your dorses like each other?"

"Horses?"

Hollie nodded.

"You know, they do," Stevie said. "I hadn't really focused on it, but they do. I guess they pick it up from us."

"No doubt," Hollie said with a dreamy look in her eyes. "So I'm dinking about some kind of classic duet. The dorses will give it a dwist. You have do have a dwist," she said meditatively. "You're nowhere without a dwist. I know!" She was so excited she half jumped off the horse blankets. "That's it. Indedible!" And then she sneezed not once, but twice.

"Listen," Stevie said, looking at her with concern, "you're getting sick. Do you think you should go home?"

"Dever," Hollie said. "I'm dabsolutely fine."

But Stevie stood up and started to pull Hollie to her feet. "You need to do something about that cold of yours."

"It's nothing," Hollie was saying. "It's dodally dover."

"Are you sure?" Stevie said doubtfully. "You sound horrible."

Hollie nodded emphatically, then gestured for Stevie to sit back down again. "I've got a great idea," she began. "You know that song 'Always'? Well, you and Phil could . . ."

Stevie obediently dropped back down on the blanket and listened to Hollie. Soon she was so absorbed in Hollie's ideas for the dressage exhibition, she forgot all about the other girl's cold.

6

THE NEXT DAY, Phil was sitting on the bench in front of the Berryville pharmacy when Stevie got off the bus.

"I've solved everything," she said while she was still halfway down the steps of the bus. "I've got our doncept."

"Doncept?" Phil said as her feet hit the dusty road.

"Oops. I've been talking to Hollie too long. I mean concept. The concept is the whole thing," Stevie told him. "Without a concept we're dead."

"For real?" Phil said as they turned up the road that led toward his place. Far off, in front of the forest, Stevie could see the red brick chimney and gray stones of his house.

"Hollie came up with this absolutely killer concept. It's a song called 'Almost.' "

"Almost what?" Phil said.

"Almost 'Almost.' I mean the name of the song is 'Almost.' Hollie and I wrote the words. It's about two people who like each other and intend to get together, but something gets in their way."

Phil looked at her blankly.

"What I mean is," Stevie went on, rushing to explain the wonderful idea to Phil, "you and I will countercanter toward each other and meet . . . almost. As we do our figure eights, we'll come closer and closer and join hands . . . almost. It's sung to the tune of 'Always.' "

"I don't know if I like the sound of this," Phil said grimly. "Miss after miss after miss sounds kind of depressing."

"But at the end . . ." Stevie turned to him and grinned.

"Yes?" said Phil, looking really interested.

"We come together for a big finale and the song changes to 'Always.' This was Hollie's idea," Stevie added hastily.

"I like the way her mind works," Phil said. They walked for a while in silence; then Phil said, "To tell you the truth, it makes me kind of nervous. Dressage and music, and riding with you. I'm wondering if Teddy and I are up to it. We aren't as experienced as you."

"So we'll practice," Stevie said happily. "I think this routine needs lots and lots of practice. Besides, it's obvious No-Name has had some dressage experience, but she may need lots of work, too."

"Okay," Phil agreed.

When Stevie entered No-Name's stall, she was afraid to look. On Friday she had doused the horse with fly spray. Today, if No-Name had hives, there would be no riding. Stevie half closed her eyes and ran her hand up No-Name's neck, relieved to find that it felt smooth.

"You're okay, you're okay," she murmured, opening her eyes. "Hey," she said in No-Name's ear, "you're not allergic to whatever is in fly spray. So the culprit must be carrots, apples, or saddle soap."

No-Name nuzzled Stevie, looking at her with her big brown eyes.

"Ready for 'Almost'?" Stevie said.

No-Name nickered.

"Me too," Stevie said. "Almost."

When No-Name was saddled, Stevie led her into the outdoor ring, where she found Phil and Teddy doing elegant serpentines. After she had mounted, Stevie sat on No-Name watching them.

Phil rode up to her and grinned. "I'm *almost* ready."

"Good attitude," Stevie said.

"The only thing is that if we're going to practice, we need the music," Phil said.

"That's okay," Stevie said. "I'll sing."

Phil raised his eyebrows, "I can hardly wait."

"Let's warm up the horses with a sitting trot and then go into a shoulder-in."

"You like to start at the top," Phil grumbled. "Teddy and I always have trouble with the shoulder-in."

"With me singing you can't miss," Stevie said cheerfully.

They walked their horses briskly around the ring to warm up their muscles, and then Stevie turned No-Name, and they trotted in opposite directions with Stevie singing.

"You belong to me . . . almost.
With a love that's free . . . almost."

Listening to herself, Stevie decided that she'd never fully appreciated her talents. She had lots of volume and expression. Next time there was a musical at the Willow Creek Community Theater, she was definitely going to try out. She could probably get a part in the chorus. Who knew? She might even be chosen to be the star.

As she and Phil rode toward each other, Stevie said,

"Reverse directions and shoulder-in." She noticed that Phil looked kind of odd, but she figured that must be because he was worried about the shoulder-in.

Doing the shoulder-in and the singing at the same time wasn't exactly easy, Stevie realized. She had to get through to No-Name that she shouldn't move just her head to the right, but her shoulder as well. If No-Name bent only her neck, she could acquire a rubber neck. Or she could throw her hind legs out so her body would be straight and there would be no shoulder curve.

Stevie pulled back gently on the right rein, but then with her right leg at the girth, she pushed No-Name forward so that her head and shoulder were moving right while her body moved forward. An average, untrained horse would fight it, but No-Name understood. Her head and right hock moved gracefully to the right while her body continued forward. She was like a ballet dancer in motion. Stevie wondered where No-Name had learned so much.

"Hey, look," came Phil's voice from the other side of the ring. Stevie looked over and saw that Teddy was doing great, switching smoothly from one side to the other.

Obviously, it was because of her singing, so Stevie sang louder. "'You belong to me . . . almost.'"

A door slammed and a woman rushed to the side of the ring. "Hi, Mrs. Marsten," Stevie called.

"Hi, Stevie," said Mrs. Marsten, patting her chest as if she were alarmed by something. "Are you all right, dear?"

"Absolutely fine," Stevie said.

"I heard the most terrible sound," Mrs. Marsten explained. "Like a creature howling in pain. I was worried that something had happened."

Stevie noticed that Phil's face had turned red. He turned away.

"We're fine." Stevie shrugged. "We're just practicing for the dressage exhibition."

"But that sound," Mrs. Marsten went on. "Whatever could it have been?"

A muffled noise burst out of Phil. Soon he was laughing so hard, he could barely talk.

"It's okay, Mom," he managed. "It was just . . . our sound effects."

"They're awfully . . ." Mrs. Marsten's words trailed off. "Do you think they're right for the exhibition?"

"We'll work on it, Mom," said Phil, now solemn-faced.

Stevie's own face was beet-red. She'd never been so embarrassed in her entire life.

After Mrs. Marsten disappeared into the house, she glared at Phil.

"Very funny!"

"Hey, I didn't tell her to say that," Phil said, but then he choked on a laugh and started coughing.

Stevie drew herself tall in the saddle and said, "You'll be glad to know that at the exhibition Lisa will be doing the singing. And Lisa has a *great* voice. She recently starred in *Annie*."

"I know," Phil said. "My whole family saw her and we thought she was fantastic."

"I guess I'm no Lisa," Stevie said grimly. "Maybe I'll be a horse-show clown. Like one of those guys in baggy pants. I seem to have a certain natural talent."

"A talent for riding, yes, for singing, no," Phil said, trotting over to her with an amused look on his face.

"Phil," came a voice from the house.

Stevie saw Mrs. Marsten's head sticking out of an upper window. "Mr. Baker called," she said, "and he wants you and Stevie to come early to the Pony Club meeting so he can check out your progress."

"No problem," Phil said, and made a thumbs-up gesture to show that everything was fine. He turned to Stevie. "We'd better groom the horses and get started."

"Definitely," Stevie said, thinking that now would be the time to try another possible allergy causer on No-Name. Today she had decided to try saddle soap.

After she'd picked No-Name's hooves, a job that Stevie liked particularly because it took gentleness and concentration, and after she had brushed and curry-combed her, Stevie went into the Marstens' tack room to polish No-Name's saddle. She put it on the saddle horse, which was a saw horse topped by a V-shaped piece of wood, and stripped the saddle, removing the girth, stirrup leathers, and irons. Then she turned the saddle over and removed the dirt and dried sweat from the lining.

She put the saddle back on the saddle horse, washed it with cold water, and dried it with a soft chamois cloth, being careful to remove all the black greasy marks that were called jockeys. Then with an almost dry sponge, using a circular motion, she put saddle soap on the seat and the flaps. From experience Stevie knew to leave neither streaks nor crumbs, but this time she used way too much soap, the way a beginner would, and left a rim of yellow soap around the edge of the stirrup flaps.

"Hey, you missed some," said Phil from behind her.

"I'm checking to see if she's allergic to saddle soap," she said.

"Good thinking," said Phil. "That might well be it."

When they got to Cross County, Mr. Baker was in the ring, practicing shoulder-ins. It was funny, Stevie thought, to see a teacher practicing. But she knew that an important part of teaching was demonstrating. Stevie sighed, thinking of some of Max's really great demonstrations, like the one he did on Prancer before the dressage rally a few weeks ago. To give good demonstrations, both horse and rider have to be in top shape. Mr. Baker and his horse were not just practicing their moves, but keeping limber.

"Stevie!" Mr. Baker said, touching his crop to his riding hat. "I'm glad you'll be joining the exhibition. Cross County riders can learn a lot from you."

Stevie smiled her thanks. "I'm sure I can learn a lot from them."

"In any case," said Mr. Baker with a smile, "I'd like to see Phil go through his paces alone first." He turned to Phil. "I know you've been working, but I have to make sure that Cross County puts on a good show in front of the members of Horse Wise. We have our honor to uphold, after all."

Stevie knew what he meant. Mr. Baker and Max Regnery were friends, but also rivals. Mr. Baker wanted to look good on his home turf.

"I'll get out of the way," Stevie said, and rode No-Name outside the ring, where she dismounted and let the horse graze on a patch of greenery next to the fence.

Phil started his dressage exercise with a sitting trot and moved into a shoulder-in and then a countercanter, making the changes with ease. He held the reins lightly while Teddy moved with his head up, feet bright, and tail lively.

"I'm impressed," Mr. Baker said when Phil was finished. "You've gained finesse." He turned to Stevie. "I think you have something to do with that."

Stevie flushed with pleasure at the compliment. "Maybe," she said, "but Phil's been working hard on his own, too."

"What will your performance consist of?" Mr. Baker asked.

"It's a dressage duet to a song called 'Almost,'" Phil said.

"Which is sung to the tune of the song 'Always,'" Stevie added.

"Is that what that tune was?" Phil asked with a smile.

Stevie ignored him. "We'll almost meet over and over again, and then at the end we will meet, and the song will change to 'Always.'"

"Very unusual—and very dramatic," Mr. Baker said with a surprised look. He glanced at his watch. "We still have a few minutes left. Why don't you show me the ending?"

"With pleasure," Stevie said, slipping off the fence and going over to No-Name. When she untied the reins from the fence, No-Name raised her head.

"Ha," she said. "I knew it."

"What?" Phil said, hurrying over on Teddy.

No-Name's head and neck were covered with hives.

"It must be the saddle soap," Stevie said.

7

"I THINK I'M getting it," Hollie said as she and Lisa walked their horses to the stable after riding class on Tuesday afternoon. "At first this lead stuff was pretty confusing, but now I think I'm catching on." She paused as she sneezed several times in a row.

"Still have that cold?" Lisa said sympathetically. Not only was Hollie's nose stuffed, but she was hoarse and her eyes were rimmed with pink. Why Hollie's mother had let her come to class when she had such a bad cold was something that Lisa couldn't understand. Her own mother would have kept Lisa in the house for days. And during rehearsals for *Annie*, Hollie had told Lisa her mother was fussy, too. In fact, having overprotective mothers was something that the girls had talked about several times.

"Does your mother know you're doing this?" Lisa said.

"What do you mean?" Hollie said. "Of course she knows I'm riding."

Lisa shook her head. "I mean, riding with such a bad cold," she explained.

"It's almost over," Hollie said, tossing her head. "It's just . . . nothing."

It didn't look like nothing to Lisa, but she decided to let the subject drop.

"Nice riding," Stevie called to Hollie as she and Carole approached the girls with their horses. "You're really getting the hang of it. Pretty soon you'll be able to try even harder moves."

"Danks," Hollie said. "I can hardly date."

"Me neither," Stevie said with a giggle. "It seems like every time Phil and I are about to get together, something happens."

"She means she can't *wait*," Lisa explained. "Hollie has a cold."

"You're still sick?" Stevie asked.

Lisa nodded. "She says it's just a tiny cold. I think she looks pretty miserable."

"Are you up to joining us at TD's?" Stevie asked Hollie.

"I'd dove to," Hollie said firmly. "I was supposed to deet my mother at the shopping center anyway."

"Great," Stevie said. "We can talk about Phil's and my dressage dancing. Are we lucky or what? We have Hollie for a songwriter and choreographer, and Lisa for a singer."

"Better her than you," said Carole with a grin, because Stevie's horrible tone-deaf singing was well-known in The Saddle Club.

Stevie feigned a hurt expression.

"Just for that I'll hide under your window and sing lullabies tonight."

Carole clutched her head and said, "The curse of the screeching soprano."

Stevie threw a handful of hay at her, and at this moment Max walked past. "What's going on?" he asked.

"I'm cleaning up," Stevie said, bending over to pick up the handful of hay. "Just making sure that everything is spick-and-span."

His eyes twinkled. "While you're at it, Stevie, make sure the tack room is spick-and-span."

The girls groaned. This meant they could forget about the trip to TD's. But then Max grinned and added, "By Saturday."

This time Stevie aimed the hay in his direction.

By the time they got to TD's, Stevie had worked out what she was going to order. "I'll have one scoop of peppermint-stick ice cream and one of rum raisin, topped with butter-crunch sauce, chocolate sprinkles, and Red Hots," she said.

The waitress sighed, wrote it down, and then turned to Hollie. "What'll it be?"

Hollie got a devilish look on her face and said, "I'll have hot dudge with a smidgen of budderscotch, dopped by a drinkle of coconud."

The waitress rolled her eyes and said, "She's even worse than you. I can't understand a word she says."

"She has a cold," Lisa said. "A very *slight* cold." She winked at Hollie, then translated for the waitress. "Hot fudge with a smidgen of butterscotch, topped by a sprinkle of coconut."

"Kill or cure," the waitress said grimly. She took Carole's and Lisa's orders and then marched off.

When she was gone, Hollie turned to Stevie and said, "I've been thinking how we could make 'Almost' even more special."

Stevie looked worried. "I wanted this to be an exhibition that no one ever forgets. But now I'm not sure No-Name and I will be able to participate." When the others looked puzzled, Stevie explained. "She broke out in hives again."

"That's terrible," Lisa said.

"Do you know what caused it?" Carole asked.

Stevie nodded. "I think so. I followed Judy Barker's directions, and I've been trying to test different possibilities. Right before No-Name broke out, I put a lot of saddle soap on her tack."

"That's a common cause of horse allergies." Carole nodded.

Stevie sighed. "You should see No-Name with welts all over her ears and head and neck. It's terrible."

"It's not such a big deal," said Hollie, sounding a bit impatient. "So she's a little allergic, so what?"

Lisa looked at Hollie with amazement. Hollie was a thoughtful person. During rehearsals for *Annie* she had been the first to help anyone who was in trouble. So why was she saying that No-Name's allergy didn't matter?

But Hollie was still thinking about the dressage exhibition. With her eyes sparkling she said, "The dressage performance should be visually memorable. Stevie and Phil have to have totally opposite looks. Their horse dance will work twice as well if it's easy to tell the two of them apart."

"Wait a second," Lisa said. Everyone stopped to stare at her. "What happened to your cold?" she said to Hollie. "You sound so much better."

"It was nothing," Hollie insisted. "I told you it would go away."

Lisa shrugged, then turned to watch the waitress set

down their orders. She thought that Hollie's cold was the strangest thing she'd ever seen. First Hollie was sneezing and rasping, and now she was perfectly normal. It didn't make any sense.

"And now for my great idea," said Hollie. "I want you and Phil to look as contrasty as possible."

"Contrasty?" Stevie echoed. "What's that?"

"It's a show-business term," said Hollie airily. "It means you and Phil should look as different as possible. Which means that you'll wear a white outfit, and Phil will wear a black one."

"Oh," Stevie said, mentally running through her horse wardrobe. "I guess I could do that, except for the boots and hat, of course. And my belt. And my cuff links. I don't have all that much white riding gear."

"We'll pull something together," Hollie said cheerfully. "Then after all the 'almosts,' you and Phil will come together and exchange coats—your white coat for his black coat—so you each wind up half black and half white. That will be a real showstopper."

"I don't know," Stevie said, not wanting to hurt Hollie's feelings, but wondering how Phil would feel about all this.

"What luck," came a voice from the doorway. "I was on my way to the supermarket and I saw you in here, Hollie. Hi, girls."

81

Hollie leaped out of her seat. "Hi, Mom. Time to go." Stuffing her riding jacket into her backpack, she hurried toward the door.

"Aren't you forgetting something?" Hollie's mother said.

"What?" Hollie looked back at The Saddle Club.

"Paying," her mother said.

"Silly me." Hollie pulled some money from her pocket, ran back to the table, and put it down. "See you guys," she said, and hurried off.

"Is Hollie's mother weird or something?" Stevie said to Lisa.

"No," Lisa said. "She's nice. Maybe a little overprotective. Like some other mothers," she added with a grin.

Stevie wrinkled her nose. "Didn't it seem as if Hollie was rushing her out of here?"

"Maybe she doesn't want her to meet *us*," Lisa said. "Maybe we're embarrassing or something."

"We're wonderful," Stevie joked, still feeling confused. There was a mystery here, and she wanted to get to the bottom of it.

"Maybe Hollie doesn't want us to meet her mother because she's afraid we'll talk to her," said Carole thoughtfully.

"About what?" Stevie said, looking at her friend.

"Didn't it seem strange that Hollie dismissed No-Name's allergy? She didn't seem at all worried."

Lisa nodded vigorously. "Hollie is one of the nicest people I know. I've never heard her sound so uncaring."

"She treated No-Name's allergy as if it were a little cold," Stevie added. "Like she talks about her own cold."

The three of them looked at each other.

"She doesn't have a cold, does she?" said Stevie as the pieces snapped together. "She has an allergy."

"To horses!" Carole exclaimed.

The Saddle Club girls sat there, dumbfounded at the sheer obviousness of the thing. When Hollie was around Pine Hollow, she sneezed, she wheezed, she was in desperate shape. As soon as she left Pine Hollow, she was fine.

"She doesn't want her mother to know she's allergic to horses," Stevie said.

"But we know," Lisa said in a soft voice. "Do you think we should do something? Should we tell someone?"

"Hollie has a good time with us," Carole said. "I think she really enjoys hanging out with The Saddle Club and learning more about horses."

Lisa nodded. "I was worried about her being lonely after *Annie* finished."

Stevie remembered how lonely and wistful Lisa had looked when she realized that *Annie* was over. For Hollie it must be even worse, Stevie thought. Lisa could go back to The Saddle Club, but Hollie didn't have anything like that. "What's the big deal?" Stevie said. "She coughs, she sniffles, she sneezes from time to time. That's nothing compared to not being able to ride."

Lisa thought of how her own mother always wanted to help but sometimes got in the way. Maybe they should tell Hollie's mother that she was allergic to horses. But if they did, Hollie would wind up embarrassed and angry.

"If Hollie wants to keep her allergy a secret, it's a secret," Lisa said firmly. "That's what friends are for."

Carole and Stevie nodded their agreement. After all, The Saddle Club always stuck together.

By Wednesday, No-Name's hives were gone. On one hand, Stevie was glad she'd be able to ride No-Name in the dressage exhibition. But on the other hand, she was disappointed she hadn't made more progress.

"It's driving me crazy," Stevie told Phil when he called the morning of the Pony Club exhibition. "I thought for sure I had the cause of No-Name's allergy nailed down, but when I tried saddle soap for the second time, just to make sure it was causing her allergy, nothing happened. She didn't break out in a single hive." She sighed.

"We're back to square one," Phil agreed.

"Oh, well," Stevie said. "At least we're ready for to-

day—unless for some reason she has another out-
break."

"Don't even say that," Phil warned. "I don't want to do
'Almost' alone. It would look kind of bizarre."

"To say the least." Stevie giggled. "A solo duet—it's a
new dressage concept."

"Can you come over early?" Phil said. "We've got a lot
to do."

"Sure," Stevie told him. Her mind was back on No-
Name and her mysterious allergies. "Isn't it strange that at
your place No-Name is always fine, but whenever we take
her somewhere, she breaks out? Maybe she hates travel-
ing."

"I don't think so," Phil said. "She doesn't seem like the
type. If it were Teddy, I could believe it. No-Name is like
you. Nothing fazes her."

"I'm fazed, believe me," Stevie said. "I'll see you in an
hour and we'll get to the bottom of this."

When Phil met Stevie at the bus stop, he looked glum.
"My parents are coming to the exhibition—if there is
one. We've got to make sure No-Name doesn't have an
allergy attack today."

"I thought about it all the way over," Stevie said. "No-
Name always seems to break out when she goes to Cross
County. But when she's there, she doesn't even go into
the stable. She waits outside, tied to the hitching post

with a lead line. What could possibly be the problem? She just stands there and munches grass."

"Can horses be allergic to grass?" Phil said.

"Maybe," Stevie said, "but if she was allergic to grass, she'd be covered with hives all the time because she's *always* eating grass."

"It's a bummer." Phil shook his head.

Stevie reached out and caught the fuzzy end of a foxtail plant from the side of the road and pulled it from the ground. She nibbled on the tender white end of the stalk. "It can't be impossible. There's got to be a way to figure this out." She blinked. "Maybe there is a way."

"What?" Phil said.

"I've got to be sure," Stevie said. "Come on, let's get over to Cross County."

The two riders had to groom their horses extra carefully for the exhibition. In dressage, it was essential for a horse and its rider to look their best. In fact, points could be lost if riders and horses looked less than perfect.

An hour later Stevie and Phil finally hit the trail for Cross County Stables.

Teddy was frisking along, his head held high. "He can tell something special's going on," Phil said. "That extra grooming always gets him going."

"Is he all right with crowds?" Stevie asked.

"He hasn't had a lot of experience with shows," Phil

admitted. "But if he gets nervous, I can always talk to him in horse latin."

Stevie grinned. Phil's method of dealing with Teddy actually seemed to work.

When they got to Cross County, bleachers had been set up outside the fence of the ring. A few younger riders who wouldn't be participating were setting up a table with cookies and lemonade.

Suddenly Stevie's stomach lurched. There were so many things that could go wrong. The duet could turn out to be a big flop, and everyone could laugh. Or Teddy could be spooked and run wild. Or, as she had been thinking all morning, No-Name could break out in hives. More than anything, Stevie wanted to do well in front of Mrs. Marsten, who must think she was a nut after hearing her sing the other day. Ever since that embarrassing moment Phil and Stevie had practiced to a tape of Lisa singing "Almost."

Phil waited for Stevie to tether No-Name in her usual spot outside the ring. Stevie shook her head and said, "We're going inside with you guys."

Once No-Name was hitched to a post where there was no grass or weeds in eating distance, Stevie went to check on that delicious patch of greenery where No-Name usually liked to munch.

Just as she thought. There was grass in No-Name's patch, but also several varieties of weeds. A horse will avoid poisonous weeds, like deadly nightshade, Stevie knew, but they will eat other weeds. Stevie examined a plant with curly green leaves and a pale-yellow flower. Could this be the culprit?

Unfortunately, Stevie decided, the only way to handle the situation was by waiting—something Stevie hated doing. The only way to make totally sure that these weeds had caused No-Name's allergy was to let her eat some. But that was something Stevie would never do without consulting Judy Barker.

"Hi, Fox," came a voice from behind her. Stevie looked over her shoulder and saw a Cross County rider who had been on the mock fox hunt that had been held at Pine Hollow several months ago. Somehow people never got tired of teasing her about being chosen to play the fox.

"Hi," Stevie said, standing up.

"How's your scent?" the boy said.

These fox jokes would be the death of her, Stevie thought. Never, ever would she be a fox again—though, in fact, she had been a fabulous fox.

"Never better," she said, letting herself into the ring. She got up on No-Name, wondering if this day was going to be one long fox joke, when she heard, "*Steeevie.*"

She looked up and saw Carole, Lisa, and Hollie. Lisa was holding the music for the duet, and Hollie had the list of dressage maneuvers they were going to perform to the strains of "Almost."

"Just a quick sound check," Hollie said, going over to the barn to check the microphone, which was in a metal wall box just inside the front door. "Testing—one, two, three, four," she said. The sound was so loud that a couple of horses jumped.

Hollie adjusted the sound and said into the mike, "Goooooooood afternoon, ladies and gentlemen."

It was funny, Stevie thought. Hollie was beginning to sound like a show-business personality.

Carole came over to Stevie and Phil and said, "The most important thing is to let the horses star. The exercises should flow out of them, as if everything were their idea."

"Like No-Name stood awake nights thinking about shoulder-ins," Stevie joked. She wanted to lighten the mood. She could see that Phil was beginning to tense under all this advice.

"Teddy's no genius," Phil said. "He's just a horse."

Carole opened her mouth, and Stevie figured that she was about to explain that in their own way horses are geniuses, which would probably make Phil even more edgy.

"Stevie," came a voice from where the cars were parked. There was something about that voice, Stevie thought, and something about that car. Yes! It was her mother's voice, and the Lake family car.

Stevie watched her parents walk across the grass and thought that it was great that her parents were there, but it would not be so great if her brothers were there, especially Michael. If Michael saw the duet, he would be singing "Almost" and teasing Stevie about Phil forever.

"Mom," Stevie said. "This is great. Did you bring—?"

"We left Michael at home," her mother said with a smile. "He's cleaning the guppy tank."

Stevie let out a sigh of relief.

"The Marstens called us and told us you choreographed and wrote the music for an exhibition number yourself," Mrs. Lake said. "It really sounds special. I'm so proud of you, Stevie."

"I had a lot of help," Stevie said.

"You'll be great," Mr. Lake said. "I've brought my camera." He raised it to show her.

Great, Stevie thought. If she and Phil messed up, it would be preserved forever on videotape. Her brothers would certainly like that.

But before she had a chance to dwell on what else could go wrong, Mr. Baker's voice boomed over the microphone, "Cross County riders and guests mount up. The Fifth Annual Cross County Dressage Exhibition is about to begin."

9

"Ms. Windsor is not a formal judge," said Mr. Baker to the assembled riders, and to their fans in the bleachers. "She is here as a commentator and friend. And we are truly honored to have her. Ms. Windsor, as I'm sure you all know, is a former member of the American equestrian team, and one of the country's leading dressage judges."

The woman Stevie recognized from the lecture at Pine Hollow took the microphone and said, "I am here only as a commentator to give advice to those who need it." She looked directly at Stevie, who was sitting on No-Name next to Phil on Teddy.

Uh-oh, Stevie thought, remembering that Hollie and

The Saddle Club had been talking and giggling during most of Ms. Windsor's talk at Pine Hollow. I'm truly a dead duck, Stevie thought. Ms. Windsor was, in fact, staring directly at Stevie, her long nose quivering with distaste.

"We'll start with a medley of dressage steps by members of Cross County and end with a duet by Phil Marsten and Stevie Lake, which incorporates these steps into a choreographed event," Mr. Baker said.

Stevie and Phil looked at each other. A choreographed event! This sounded like a big deal.

Music blared from the public-address system as three Cross County horses and riders entered the ring.

"Riders will demonstrate the countercanter," Mr. Baker explained.

The horses cantered to the left with their right legs leading. This was the opposite of what they instinctively wanted to do. At first the horses and riders showed great skill, but then one horse broke into a disunited canter.

In a disunited canter a horse has his left legs tucked under him and his right legs spread in full gallop position. This is one of the silliest-looking things a horse can do. It's also dangerous because a horse can easily lose its balance.

Carole watched the disunited canter and shook her

head. "Once one horse gets off the gait, the rest will go too."

Sure enough, the second horse broke into a disunited canter and then the third.

Abruptly the music stopped and Mr. Baker spoke over the microphone, "That was a good beginning. A few more practice sessions and the horses will have it. Perhaps Ms. Windsor has something to say." He passed the microphone to Ms. Windsor.

"A fine attempt," Ms. Windsor said. "I can see that this Pony Club takes dressage seriously."

Stevie was surprised the woman didn't say more. Maybe she was saving her most critical comments for Stevie and Phil.

The next demonstration was of the serpentine. This time the horses and riders rose to the occasion, weaving around the edge of the ring with grace and speed. After that five horses pirouetted to the left and then to the right. Stevie noticed that Mr. Baker looked very pleased.

And then the whole of Cross County did left half passes and right half passes, getting their horses to walk sideways by crossing their legs. As they backed toward the center, so that together the horses looked like the rays of a sun, the audience burst into applause. Ms. Windsor took the microphone and said, "A very creditable exhibition.

A Pony Club shows its true stamina and class when it refuses to let itself be daunted by an initial mishap."

There was a pause while the audience digested this thought, and then there was a round of applause.

"And now Stevie Lake and Phil Marsten will perform a dressage duet to the music of"—Mr. Baker looked at the slip of paper in his hand more closely—" 'Almost,' which will be sung by Lisa Atwood, the star of a recent local production of *Annie*."

Stevie swallowed. Never had she been in an exhibition when there were so many uncertainties. For a second— just a second—Stevie wished that her parents weren't there. Her father was smiling proudly and had his camera raised.

But then Stevie looked over at Max, who was standing at the rail next to Mr. Baker. Max's blue eyes seemed to be staring right into her, making her calm.

Lisa sang,

"You belong to me . . . almost."

Stevie and Phil raised their hats to each other and rode in opposite directions in a sitting trot. They met on the word "almost" and leaned toward each other, almost touching. Then they headed into a serpentine, and when they neared each other, they reached out their hands, barely missing on the word "almost." The crowd was into it now, laughing and clapping. Phil and Stevie spun off into giant figure eights that got smaller and smaller and closer and closer, until it seemed as if they were about to fall into each other's arms. Again, at the word "almost," they missed and spun off into revolving pivots. As their horses met at the opposite end of the ring, they slid into a countercanter, moving gracefully back around the ring.

Lisa sang,

"With a love that's free . . . almost."

The smoothness of No-Name's canter and the swell of Lisa's voice was exhilarating. As Stevie and Phil moved toward one another for the final time, Stevie raised her arm, ready to join hands with Phil. Phil raised his arms. The crowd cheered. Stevie and Phil reached for each other so they could hold hands.

Excited by the applause, No-Name did a perfect *piaffe*. Seeing her, Teddy started a *piaffe* of his own. Next thing Stevie knew, she and Phil were waving their arms, trying to keep their balance. In the stands Stevie could see the horrible black eye of her father's camera. This disaster was being recorded for posterity.

A terrible silence hung over the ring. Then Lisa, show-business veteran that she was, sang,

"Almost!"

It brought down the house. The people in the bleachers stood up, cheering and laughing. Stevie's parents made victory signs. Even Mr. Baker was smiling. By this time Phil had gotten Teddy under control and Stevie was upright in the saddle. Phil rode back to Stevie and took her hand, and when the two of them raised their hands, everyone cheered louder.

"I'm speechless," Mr. Baker said over the microphone. "I'm going to turn for comment to Ms. Windsor."

Here goes nothing, Stevie thought.

Ms. Windsor took a deep breath.

Stevie looked at Phil and whispered, "Prepare to die."

"I have witnessed many exhibitions of so-called horse dancing," Ms. Windsor said, "and as a rule I tend to turn a disapproving eye on them."

"I bet," Stevie whispered to Phil.

"But I must say that this one was remarkably lively, and the ending did make me smile."

Stevie looked at Ms. Windsor. Could it be true? Yes, Stevie saw that under her long, dour nose, Ms. Windsor was actually smiling.

"Congratulations to Stevie Lake and Phil Marsten," Mr. Baker said, looking intensely relieved. " 'Almost' will be remembered at Cross County for a long time."

"We had a lot of help," Stevie said, but since no one could hear her, Mr. Baker motioned her over to the microphone. "We had a lot of help," she said, hearing her voice boom to the crowd. "As you all know, the singing was done by Lisa Atwood." There was a round of applause for Lisa's great singing. "The concept, choreography, and songwriting were done by Hollie Bright." For her there was an even bigger round of applause.

"Where do you get your great ideas?" someone called.

Stevie carried the microphone over to Hollie, who sneezed loudly.

A puzzled silence followed. Stevie said hastily, "I think Hollie got her concept from Phil and me." She looked over at Phil. "I guess she thinks we're 'almost' kind of people."

This raised a laugh, but Mr. Baker stretched out his hand for the microphone and said, "Stevie's too modest. I'm sure that none of you realize it, but the horse she's riding is a talented but difficult horse. We had . . ."

"No-Name," Stevie supplied. "Her name is No-Name."

"How unusual," Mr. Baker said with a smile. "In any case we had No-Name at Cross County for a couple of weeks, and we liked her, but those were difficult weeks. She kept coming down with hives, and we couldn't track down the cause of them. And although she's an intelligent, spirited horse, she isn't easy to handle. So I think we all owe Stevie an extra hand for bringing No-Name to the exhibition with no hives and no discipline problems."

If only he knew, Stevie thought. That final *piaffe* hadn't exactly been part of the plan.

As the audience applauded, Stevie sneaked a look over to the stands and saw that Mr. Lake was getting all this on tape. Now Stevie couldn't wait until her brothers saw it.

"With Stevie and No-Name I think we see a perfect rider-horse combination," Mr. Baker said. "Can anyone guess why this is so?"

Carole, sitting in the stand, raised her hand and said, "Because they're so much alike?"

Mr. Baker nodded. "Good horse-and-rider combinations are often like that. They understand each other because they're so similar. What you want to watch out for are opposites, like a bullying rider and a timid horse. Or a bullying horse and a timid rider."

The crowd laughed.

"At any rate, I'd like to thank Ms. Windsor for her contribution to this event," Mr. Baker said, "and also the riders from Pine Hollow."

"What a day," Stevie said, turning to Phil. "I didn't think things would turn out so well." But then suddenly she remembered that she'd forgotten about Teddy. "Is he okay?" she said, looking down at him.

"Teddy's fine," Phil said. "He can tell that everyone is happy, so he's happy."

"You know the best thing of all?" Stevie said happily to Phil.

"What?"

"No hives," she said, pointing to No-Name's neck. "Not one."

Phil leaned over, checking No-Name's ears and face, especially the upside-down white exclamation point that ran up her nose. "You're right." He looked up at Stevie. "You've figured it out, haven't you?"

"I think so," Stevie said. "You see that green patch outside the fence? That's where I used to tie No-Name. But today I didn't, and I checked and it's full of weeds."

"That would do it," Phil said. "That green spot must look like a splendid feast to her."

"Poor No-Name," Stevie said, nodding. "It's like being allergic to fudge sauce."

"That's where you two are not alike," Phil said with a grin.

"Nice work, Stevie," said Mr. Baker, coming over. "I've had a few rides on No-Name myself, so I can appreciate what you were up against. You got her under control without making her feel angry or oppressed."

"Who could oppress a horse with an exclamation point on her nose?" Stevie asked. When Mr. Baker smiled, she added, "You know, I think I've found what No-Name is allergic to."

"What?" Mr. Baker said.

"Something in that patch of weeds over there." She pointed to the weeds outside the fence.

"That could be," Mr. Baker said thoughtfully. "It's not uncommon for horses to be allergic to weeds. I'll get rid of that patch right away. Thanks, Stevie."

Mr. and Mrs. Lake appeared next to Stevie, looking proud and happy. "You were great," Mr. Lake said. "That ending was pure genius."

Stevie and Phil looked at each other and grinned.

"Not only was Stevie great in the performance," Mr. Baker said, "but she's tracked down her mount's allergy."

Everyone was looking at Stevie, so she figured that she might as well explain. "I took a scientific approach and tried one possible allergen at a time. The first time I tried fly spray, which is the most common cause of horse allergies. The next time I tried saddle soap."

By then a crowd had gathered around Stevie. It included Hollie, Carole, and Lisa, as well as Phil's parents and his younger sister, Rachel. Naturally, Mr. Lake was taping the whole thing.

"But neither of those was the culprit," Stevie said, truly enjoying herself because her parents seemed to be bug-eyed with wonder at this new responsible, scientific Stevie. "So I made a mental list of the times No-Name came down with hives, and I realized that each time she had just visited Cross County."

Stevie noticed Mrs. Marsten give Rachel a nudge. Phil saw it, too, and he looked over at Stevie and gave her a small nod, as if to say—lay it on.

"So I thought of all the things No-Name had done at Cross County, and I realized that she hadn't been inside the barn, so it must have been something outside. And she had come fully saddled, so it couldn't be tack. So it must have been something outside, probably something she ate. And then I had this memory of her munching those weeds over there."

"Big deal," Rachel said softly.

"It *is* a big deal, Rachel," Mrs. Marsten said. "Those hives can be life threatening to No-Name."

"I'm proud of you, Stevie," Mrs. Lake said. "This makes me realize that you're on your way to being a responsible adult."

"Hey, not so fast," Stevie joked. "I'm not so sure I'm ready to be a responsible adult."

"I can just see it," Mrs. Lake said dreamily to her husband. "Stevie arguing a case in front of the Supreme Court." The Lakes were both lawyers.

"Sorry." Stevie shook her head. "I've already got my plans made. I'm going to be a horse detective."

"That's it," Mr. Lake said. When everyone turned to look at him, he explained, "That's going to be the title of this videotape: *Stevie Lake: Horse Detective*."

"How did you raise Stevie so well?" Mrs. Marsten asked Mrs. Lake. "She's so mature and thoughtful."

"Oh, we just did what comes naturally," Mrs. Lake said airily. "We followed our instincts."

"And prayed a lot," Mr. Lake added.

This broke the ice. In a second the Lakes and Marstens were smiling at each other—with the exception of Rachel, who said, "You think I want to turn out to be a creep like her?"

"Rachel, dear," Mrs. Marsten said, "I have the feeling your chickens are getting hungry." She looked at her watch. "And this time of day they're probably laying eggs."

"I'm out of here," Rachel said, and streaked out of the ring toward the Marstens' home.

"Would you like to join us for lunch?" Mrs. Marsten said to the Lakes.

"There's a new Japanese restaurant in the shopping center," Mrs. Lake said.

"I love sushi," Mrs. Marsten said.

Mr. Marsten and Mr. Lake looked at each other with dismay.

"I don't know why," Mr. Lake said, "but I'm just not in the mood for raw fish today."

"Strange, isn't it? Me neither," said Mr. Marsten with a grin. "Usually I'm dying for raw fish, but right now I'm just not in the mood."

"How about a hamburger?" Mr. Lake suggested.

"And fries," Mr. Marsten said, brightening. "And onion rings. Watching all that exercise made me hungry."

Mrs. Lake turned to Phil and Stevie and said, "How long will it take you two to get ready?"

But Stevie didn't want to stop riding, and when she looked at Phil, she saw that he felt the same way. "We're not dressed for a restaurant," she said. "Do you suppose we could stay and ride?"

"After a performance like that I don't see why not," Mrs. Lake said.

As Stevie and Phil headed toward Mr. Baker to get his

permission to go trail riding, she said, "You know, I've got to try being responsible again sometime. It really goes over well."

"Don't overdo it," Phil said. "I like you just the way you are."

Mr. Baker said that not only would it be fine for Phil and Stevie to ride on the trails behind Cross County, but that he would be glad to supply horses for Carole, Lisa, and Hollie, too. At that moment Phil's redheaded friend, A.J., appeared and asked if he could join, so they made up a party of six.

As soon as everyone was saddled up, Phil led the way to a road that curved through a harvested oat field that was now nothing but brown stubble with shoots of tender new weeds. Knowing that this was exactly the kind of delicacy that No-Name liked—and shouldn't have—Stevie kept a close rein on her. Soon they entered the forest, slipping into the cool, leafy shade of the oak trees, seeing the haze of spiderwebs over the trail.

It was the first time all day that Stevie hadn't been on edge. She felt her neck relax, and then her back, and then her legs. Off to the left she could hear the hum of a brook. This was what riding was all about. Practice and exhibitions were great, but the best moments were when horses and riders were wandering through the countryside, free to do whatever they wanted.

They came to a clearing, and Stevie looked up from her reverie to see that this field wasn't like the fields around Pine Hollow. It had a fierce outcropping of rock near the top, and the jagged shape of the grassy slope showed that this wasn't a hill, but a foothill of the Silverado Mountains.

Phil stopped Teddy and raised his hand for the riders to gather around him. "I know you're used to the country around Pine Hollow," he said, "so I have to warn you that under the grass there are rocks, and in the bushes there are ravines. Be sure to stay on the trail because the footing here is full of surprises." He looked from one rider to the next to make sure that they understood. His gaze rested on Hollie.

"I've dot it," she said. "I'll stay dight on the drail."

The others laughed, but The Saddle Club also exchanged looks. Obviously, Hollie's allergies were back.

"Okay," Phil said. "Let's go."

He turned, and Teddy took off along the road, which was filled with tufts of grass. No-Name raised her head as if at last the fun was beginning and took off after Teddy in a beautiful gallop, with long, light steps. It was like floating, Stevie thought, or being a butterfly. As they entered the woods, climbing the stony mountain slope, dark hemlock branches brushed Stevie's arms.

Phil and Teddy disappeared over a rise, and No-Name,

taking huge steps, scarcely working at all, followed into what looked like a giant saucer filled with silver grass.

Phil raised his hand. "If you're really quiet, you can hear the wind grass singing." Stevie knew that this was a kind of grass that grew only in windy, exposed places. The funny thing about wind grass was that sometimes its dry blades picked up the sound of the wind.

The riders closed their eyes. At first all Stevie could hear was the whine of a jet plane overhead. Then it came, a sound halfway between a buzz and a song.

Stevie giggled. For some reason the sound of wind grass made her nose itch.

Phil pointed to a slow gray ribbon that wound itself through the green fields below. "That's the Silverado River," he said to Hollie.

"It's fantastic," she said. But she didn't sound right. The words came out slowly and painfully, as if she had to force them.

"Are you okay?" Stevie asked.

Hollie didn't respond at first. Instead she was taking shallow breaths that didn't seem to satisfy her.

"I'm dine!" Hollie said, and from the way she said it, with a toss of her head, Stevie knew that she was trying to raise a laugh. But there was nothing to laugh at, because Hollie had turned pale, with faint blue shadows under her eyes.

A.J.'s expression was concerned. "You look like you're going to faint."

"It's her horse allergy," Stevie said. She reached across to put her hand on Hollie's face, feeling its clammy sweat. "You're allergic to horses, aren't you, Hollie? Tell me the truth."

But Hollie's eyes were glassy and vague, and her skin was getting paler.

"Can you hear me?" Stevie shouted. "Hollie!"

Hollie focused on her and whispered, "Yes." It came out as a horrible wheezing sound.

Stevie remembered what Judy Barker had said about allergic asthma. Suddenly Hollie's "cold" wasn't funny. It might even be deadly.

"We've got to get her back," Carole said. "She's got to go to the hospital."

Stevie glanced around anxiously. She knew that Carole was right, but the only way to get Hollie back was on a horse, and Hollie was allergic to horses. Still, that was their only option.

"Help me put her on No-Name," Stevie called to Phil. "I've got to move her fast."

Phil started to say something, and she knew that he was thinking that No-Name was an untested horse—who knew how she'd react to a second rider? But then Phil, sitting on Teddy, gently put his arms around Hollie and lifted her off her horse while Carole, who had dismounted, held Hollie's legs. They slid her onto No-Name in front of Stevie. The girl was too weak to protest.

With her arms supporting Hollie, Stevie pressed in with her knees.

Immediately No-Name understood. She was off, stumbling down the trail, her shoes hitting a rock so hard, they sent off sparks. A hollow in the trail filled with spongy ground slowed No-Name to a stumble.

This isn't fast enough, Stevie thought, trying not to panic. With her left knee she pressed No-Name lightly.

No-Name headed into a hemlock forest that was dark and tangled underfoot. For a second No-Name balked, but then she cantered over the dark ground, head down, dodging trees.

"Hollie," Stevie said, shaking her, "stay awake. Don't give up. I need you."

Hollie wheezed something that Stevie couldn't understand.

Stevie looked up and saw that No-Name was headed straight for a tree. At the last second the horse bent left— a real dressage move—saving them all.

"Stay calm," Stevie told Hollie. "Make yourself be calm. Think of something. Think of . . ." But Stevie couldn't think of what to think of.

No-Name was falling, feet caught in an avalanche of

stones, but without changing direction or losing speed, she angled onto the hard ground next to the trail in a perfect shoulder-in.

They came to a stone fence, and No-Name easily soared over it.

"You'll be okay," Stevie said to Hollie. "Think . . . dressage." She knew it was ridiculous, but it was all Stevie could think of.

From Hollie there came something that felt like a strangled hiccup.

No-Name stopped with a jolt. They were on a high bank, looking down at a creek twelve feet below.

Stevie slumped. This was hopeless. Hollie could die in her arms. But then No-Name was loping along the fragile bank in a perfect countercanter.

Thorns tore at Stevie's boot. One of them ripped through the knee of her breeches.

Hollie stirred. "Think countercanter," Stevie said, not knowing what she was saying anymore, just talking to talk.

A gurgle came from Hollie. Stevie leaned forward to look at her and saw that the blue circles and swelling around her eyes had spread. She raised a hand to touch Hollie's face and felt that it was cold.

"We're almost there," she said, desperately trying not to think about the rest of the ride.

No-Name pulled out of the thorn bushes, and Stevie heard the soft gurgling of the stream. It was easy now, she thought. They could follow the stream.

But the stream was eight feet deep, and there was no way around it.

No-Name plunged in, swimming left around a mossy green boulder and then right through a pool so smooth, it seemed invisible.

"Hollie," she whispered. "Are you okay? Are you with me? No-Name is doing a figure eight."

Hollie choked.

No-Name's feet hit pebbles of the bank with a crunch. She got her footing and scrambled onto the far bank. Stevie looked downhill. There was a field of soggy brown earth and hay bales. This was the worst kind of footing.

"Think serpentine," Stevie said to No-Name as she held tight to Hollie.

Swerving from side to side, as Stevie fought to keep her seat, No-Name crossed the field, feet sliding, white foam flecking her neck, head high and proud. Finally, exhausted and relieved, she drew up amid a swirl of stones in front of the Cross County barn.

"Someone," Stevie yelled. "Someone come."

Silence. Everyone must have gone for lunch after the exhibition.

"Help!" Stevie screamed again. "Help!"

Carefully, gently, Stevie lowered Hollie from No-Name's back. "Stand," she begged Hollie. "Please." But Hollie couldn't stand, so Stevie had to let her sag onto the grass.

Stevie jumped down and looked into Hollie's face. Her eyelids were fluttering and her eyes were unfocused while her breath came out in horrible rasps.

There was a clatter. Stevie looked up to see Carole and Phil riding to the barn.

"Call an ambulance and see if you can find Mr. Baker," Stevie said to Phil, and to Carole she said, "Get the first-aid kit."

Carole was startled that Stevie wanted a bandage at a time like this, but she tethered her horse and ran.

Stevie looked at Hollie's fluttering eyelids and knew that more than anything she had to get her away from the horses. She quickly tethered No-Name to the fence and ran back to Hollie.

"Can you stand?" she said, raising Hollie to a kneeling position and putting her arm around her shoulder. Hollie didn't answer, so Stevie half carried, half dragged her away from the barn and horses.

Lisa and A.J. came cantering out of the forest.

"How is she?" Lisa said.

"I don't know. Max must be back. Tell him to get Hollie's parents." Stevie was holding Hollie's head in her lap.

Hollie's breathing was coming in shorter and shorter rasps, which sounded as if no air at all was getting to her lungs.

Carole ran out of the barn with the red, white, and blue first-aid kit. She handed it to Stevie.

Stevie opened the box and scrambled through the contents, scattering bandages and creams on the ground. Then she found what she wanted. She pulled out the EpiPen. She broke it open and gave Hollie a shot, remembering the instructions that Judy Barker had given her several weeks ago.

Hollie's eyelids fluttered and she wheezed continuously, gasping for air.

"Come on, Hollie," Stevie prayed out loud. "This is medicine. You'll be better in a few minutes, you'll see."

From the bottom of the hill came the scream of an ambulance siren.

"WHAT'S GOING ON?" Hollie whispered, staring at the crowd of worried riders surrounding her.

"You nearly died," Stevie said grimly. "That's all. Don't try to talk—okay?"

Hollie shook her head and sat up, still breathing with effort. But the swelling and circles under her eyes were fading slowly, and her lips were pink instead of blue, and slowly her wheezing eased.

The ambulance whizzed around the corner. Two men in white jumped out and ran over to Hollie.

"I'm okay," she said to them. She made a movement to get up, then sank back, exhausted.

One of the men in white took out a stethoscope to

listen to her breathing, while Stevie showed the other one the EpiPen she'd given Hollie.

"That was a good move," the ambulance attendant said to her. "I think you saved your friend's life."

A car came speeding around the corner of the barn, and Hollie's parents jumped out. Hollie's mother ran over to her and put a hand on her cheek.

"Max and Mr. Baker are on their way," Lisa said.

Looking up at her mother, Hollie said, "I'm okay. Thanks to Stevie."

Hollie's mother looked at the ambulance attendant, who said, "The wheezing in her lungs is down, but we have to take her to the hospital." He turned to Hollie and said, "Can you walk?"

"Of course I can," Hollie said indignantly. But when she tried to stand, she wobbled.

"She's exhausted from the attack," the attendant said to her mother. With the attendant on one side and her mother on the other, Hollie walked slowly to the ambulance.

In silence Stevie, Lisa, Carole, Phil, and A.J. watched them. Now that the danger was past, Stevie suddenly felt weak. Her knees wobbled and her hands trembled. All she could think about was Hollie's turning blue. Stevie didn't know much about allergies—especially not before the last few weeks—but she knew enough to sense that

Hollie had been in big trouble. Hollie owed her life both to a miracle and to No-Name's unbelievable skills. Tears streamed down Stevie's face.

"You were great, Stevie," Phil said, putting an arm around her. "You saved Hollie's life."

"How did you know what to do?" A.J. asked.

Stevie brushed away the tears. "I guess I was so into horse allergies that I learned something about human allergies," she said. "Imagine." She was stunned. She had spent the last few weeks trying to save No-Name's life, and yet when the danger came, it was Hollie who needed her help.

"Hollie was lucky you were there," Phil said softly.

Which brought up the thought that had been hovering at the edge of Stevie's mind.

She looked at Lisa and Carole. "None of this would have happened if we'd told Hollie's mother she was allergic to horses."

Lisa nodded solemnly. "We knew how dangerous allergies are to horses. We should have known they're just as dangerous for humans."

"Especially me," Stevie said. "I was the supposed expert. I keep thinking about how I laughed when Hollie talked through her nose. Boy, was that funny," she said miserably. "You could die laughing at a joke like that."

A battered brown station wagon pulled up, and Mr. Baker got out with Max. The five riders ran over to them.

"I nearly killed Hollie," Stevie said to Max.

"Hey, settle down, start from the beginning," Max said.

"It all started with *Annie*," Stevie said.

"I can see this is going to take a while," Max said, leaning against the fence.

Ten minutes later, when the Lakes and the Marstens returned from lunch, Stevie was calmer, her hands had stopped shaking, and she was no longer convinced that she was a monster.

"You'll be proud of your daughter when you hear what happened," Max said. He told them about Hollie's asthma attack and pointed out that most people wouldn't have had the presence of mind to handle things as well as Stevie had.

"You're wonderful!" Mrs. Lake said.

"I'm proud of you," Mr. Lake said.

No-Name let out a loud whinny.

Stevie couldn't believe that she had forgotten about No-Name, who was tethered to the fence, looking longingly at the forbidden patch of weeds. Stevie rushed over and hugged the beautiful horse.

"Forget about eating weeds," she said to No-Name. "I'm going to have to watch you like a hawk from now

119

on. But you're a hero, No-Name. You saved Hollie's life. If you weren't such a great dressage horse, she would have died in the woods." She untied No-Name's reins and led her over to the mounting block so she could ride her back to Phil's place.

Stevie's legs seemed unusually heavy, and her feet seemed to have turned into lead weights. Max was next to her, saying, "After a ride like that, your body goes into low gear so that it can rest and refuel itself."

"At least Hollie's okay," Stevie said as she lifted her leg over the saddle, thinking that if she was this tired, Hollie must be totally drained.

Stevie and Phil rode the short distance to Phil's house in silence. When they reached the gate of the Marstens' place, Phil glanced at her. "This has been some day," he said.

"Terrible and great," Stevie agreed. "Max said that when he phoned the hospital, he found out Hollie had been treated and released. What a relief."

"I'll say." Phil shook his head.

In the stable Stevie took her time brushing and combing No-Name. It felt simple and relaxing to groom the mare. From running through the forest and swimming downstream, her coat was filthy. Stevie tenderly brushed willow leaves and milkweed silk from her mane. "You

120

were great today," she whispered. "It takes a champion to do what you did."

Stevie wondered where No-Name had gotten those amazing dressage skills she had shown in the race back to the barn. It had been pretty funny, she realized, that she had thought that she could teach No-Name a thing or two. Obviously, No-Name had been trained to be a champion. But by whom? And where? The more she got to know this beautiful horse, the more of a mystery she became.

Stevie looked at No-Name's eyes to see if she was listening, but No-Name's lids were drifting downward, and it seemed that she was taking a catnap, or rather a horsenap. Stevie figured that No-Name must be even more tired than she was.

Her parents had driven to the Marstens' house, so after No-Name had been untacked and groomed, they bundled Stevie into the back of the car. As soon as the car started, Stevie felt groggy. She wasn't much of a napper. In fact, usually she thought that naps were an incredible waste of time. But today . . .

"So what do you think of No-Name?" Mr. Lake said.

"I couldn't have done it without her," Stevie said, snapping back into alertness. "No-Name is the greatest. Mr. Baker can take her back and keep her with the other horses at Cross County now that he knows what makes her allergic." The thought of someone else riding No-Name made Stevie miserable, but the dressage exhibition was over, and her allergy problem was solved. Stevie had played her part. Now it was time to step aside. "Of course," she went on sadly, "she's a lot of horse, and it will take a strong-willed rider to control her, but I'm sure he'll find someone when he's ready to sell her."

"Strong-willed, hmmmmm?" Mr. Lake mused.

"Yup," said Stevie. "She needs someone who won't put up with any attitude from her, and who loves her and knows where her best tickle spot is, and who will keep training her in dressage, and . . ." Stevie's words trailed off because suddenly she was feeling sad. She had been dreaming of having her own horse for such a long time. And while they were together, she and No-Name had seemed like the perfect pair.

"I'm glad you like her because we just bought her for you from Mr. Baker," her father said.

"What?"

Mrs. Lake turned around to face her daughter. "She's yours, honey. We know how much you've been wanting a horse of your own. After seeing your performance on her today, and hearing about her role in Hollie's rescue, your father and I agreed that we couldn't think of a better horse for you to own."

It took a moment for her mother's words to register.

And another moment for Stevie to swallow the incredible joy that was gathering in her throat.

When she could finally speak, it wasn't to say anything special—only to shriek so loudly, it could be heard for three counties.

"ARE YOU ALL right?" Carole asked as Stevie walked into the tack room five minutes ahead of time.

"Why shouldn't I be?" Stevie said.

Carole looked at her watch. "Because you're early. This is . . . not you, Stevie." For a second Carole wondered if Stevie had let all the talk about her maturity go to her head. But then from the gloomy way Stevie was pacing around the tack room, Carole guessed that it was something else.

"I talked to Hollie's mother, and she's looking forward to seeing us," Lisa said.

"That's great," Stevie said miserably. "She's probably looking forward to seeing us so that she can give us a piece of her mind. After all, if The Saddle Club had been a true friend to Hollie, we would have stopped her from riding."

"You're in a gloomy mood," Lisa said.

"I should think you'd be happy," Carole said. "When you think about it, you're in luck."

"How did you know?" Stevie said, looking at her with amazement.

"Know what?" said Carole, realizing that there was something going on that she didn't understand.

"That my parents bought me No-Name," Stevie said.

Lisa and Carole jumped, shrieking with joy, and put their arms around Stevie.

"I can't believe it," Lisa exclaimed. "I'm so happy."

"No-Name is the horse for you," Carole added. "You're perfect for each other."

"So tell us everything," Lisa said.

"I don't think I deserve her," Stevie said sadly.

"Come on, Stevie," Carole said. "You know you've been dying to have your own horse, and you know that No-Name is just right for you."

Stevie flopped down on the pile of blankets and said, "I couldn't believe it. My parents bought her as a surprise for me. And now"—Stevie took a deep breath—"the Marstens are driving her over in their van this afternoon. Max has a stall picked out for her. He's even got a nameplate waiting for her—all I have to do is tell him her name."

"Unbelievable." Carole sighed. "It's as romantic as the way I got Starlight."

"That's true," Stevie said. Carole had gotten Starlight on Christmas Eve—talk about great Christmas presents!

"So why aren't you thrilled?" Carole said.

Stevie looked glumly at them. "I *was* thrilled. But then I stayed up all night thinking about this. My parents are rewarding me for being responsible, but if I were really responsible, Hollie wouldn't have gotten sick in the first place. I keep thinking that this is some kind of terrible trade—Hollie nearly dies and I get a horse."

Lisa stretched out her legs and looked at her boots. "I keep thinking of how Hollie showed me the ropes when I joined the company of *Annie*. She saved me from a lot of mistakes, so what did I do? I let her put herself in danger."

"The Saddle Club was not at its best," Carole agreed. "I kept telling myself that I didn't realize how dangerous allergies can be, but I knew."

"Great," Stevie said, stretching out her legs so that she, too, was staring at her boots. Now all three members of The Saddle Club were staring dejectedly at their feet.

"There's only one thing to do, and that's tell Hollie how sorry we are," Stevie said. Slowly, she stood up. Slowly, Lisa and Carole stood up.

126

They walked through the woods to Hollie's house, and the walk, which usually would have been filled with horse talk and future plans, was silent and miserable.

By the time they got to Hollie's front door, they half expected Hollie's mother to be angry at them. Instead, she smiled and said, "Ever since you called and said you'd be coming over, Hollie has been looking forward to it. She won't be really well until she sees you."

They climbed the stairs to Hollie's bedroom, which had white ruffled curtains at the window and a huge white comforter on the bed. Looking small and pale, Hollie was sitting up in bed.

"I'm really sorry," Stevie started. "I couldn't sleep. It's all my fault."

"I was supposed to look out for you," Lisa said.

But Hollie shook her head so hard, spots of color rose to her cheeks. "There are some things you can't trade away," she said firmly, "and one of those is responsibility for your own health. I knew I had allergies. I'm allergic to lots of things. I was allergic to the makeup in the show."

"That's why you took it off so fast," said Lisa, thinking back to Hollie in front of the makeup mirror.

Hollie nodded. "I wanted to be in the play so much. Just like I wanted to ride with The Saddle Club."

"We knew you were allergic," Stevie said in a low

voice. "We figured it out and we didn't do anything about it. That's the thing we can't forget."

But Hollie shook her head. "Allergies are the responsibility of the person who has them, Stevie."

"I don't know," Stevie said, looking totally unconvinced. "I still think we should have done something."

"Listen," Hollie said, "do you know what can make a serious asthma attack even worse?"

"Stress," Stevie said.

"That's right," Hollie replied. "And I was getting more and more tense. I could feel my lungs getting tighter and tighter until you started saying those really crazy things."

"Like what?" said Stevie, totally mystified.

"You were yelling 'Great shoulder-in' or something like that."

Stevie felt her face grow red.

"And you were yelling 'What a countercanter,' " Hollie added. "When I heard you yelling all those nutty horse things, it helped keep my mind off the asthma attack."

"Really?" Stevie said.

"It was so crazy," Hollie went on. "You really saved me, Stevie. I was too focused on what you'd say next to get tense."

"Being a horse nut really has some advantages," Carole said with a grin.

"Thanks a million," Stevie said, her face pink.

"Actually, you know what this proves," said Carole, standing and raising her finger, as if she were about to make a cosmically important point.

Stevie, Lisa, and Hollie shook their heads.

"That you can never be too crazy about horses," Carole said.

"Right!" Stevie and Lisa said together.

There was a sudden silence as the Saddle Club members realized that this didn't apply to Hollie. In fact, being horse crazy was dangerous for her.

But Hollie shook her head. "I promised my mother not to do any more silly things, but my riding days may not be over. The doctors can try to desensitize me to horses by giving me small doses of horse allergen."

"A horse shot?" Stevie asked.

"Something like that," Hollie said. "And on top of that I can take premedication—that is, I can use an antihistamine and a bronchodilator whenever I know I'm going to be around horses."

"Sounds complicated," Stevie said, looking worried again.

"It is, and until we get everything worked out right, I'm going to have to stay away from the stable."

"But we won't have to stay away from you," Lisa said. "And your house is just a walk through the woods from Pine Hollow, so we'll be seeing a lot of you."

"I hope," Hollie said, "because I've got this brand-new concept. All we need is thirty horses—with the riders dressed in green and orange and purple, carrying torches. I'm thinking we could do it at night. It would be great with a rock-and-roll band . . . and then maybe a few clowns."

The members of The Saddle Club grinned at each other—Hollie was her old self again.

13

"THEY'RE LOST," Stevie said.

"They can't be lost," Carole said. "They've been here a hundred times before."

"Then they were in an accident," Stevie insisted.

"They're not even late," Lisa said, looking at her watch.

"Then your watch is broken," Stevie said.

Momentarily shaken, Lisa put her watch to her ear, because even to her it seemed as if the Marstens were taking unimaginably long.

"No-Name has been kidnapped. . . ." Stevie began. But at this moment they heard the familiar sputtering cough of the Marstens' car. And then from around the corner came the Marsten station wagon, pulling after it the Marsten red, white, brown, and rust horse trailer, which was even older than their station wagon.

"No-Name," Stevie whispered.

The station wagon stopped and Phil jumped out of the passenger side. "Here she is," he called.

Stevie walked slowly toward the trailer, as if she were in a trance. And part of her did feel as if she were dreaming. "Is she all right?" she said to Phil. "Nothing happened on the way over?"

"Stevie Lake," Phil said with a grin, "you sound like a true horse owner. No-Name is fine."

Stevie unhooked the back of the horse trailer. "It's me, kid, no fancy stuff, now," she said, knowing that some horses are driven absolutely crazy by a ride in a trailer.

No-Name, however, seemed perfectly calm. Stevie slipped toward her head, saying, "I've got a surprise for you, and the surprise is"—she reached No-Name's head— "me! You're mine. I'm yours." She put her nose next to No-Name's nose, and they nuzzled each other.

From the clanking in the rear Stevie could tell that Phil was getting the ramp in place. "Ready," he called.

"You're going to like it here," Stevie told the mare, backing her out gently. "Pine Hollow is the best spot on earth." No-Name's hind legs were on the ramp now, and her rear quarters were moving downward. This was a moment when a horse was likely to spook, but No-Name seemed perfectly calm, as if she'd done this a hundred times before.

Near the rear of the trailer Carole and Lisa were holding up a sign that said:

WELCOME NO-NAME

Stevie had to laugh because this was one of the sillier signs she had ever seen. Then, without warning, the letters on the sign blurred. Stevie wiped the tears from her eyes. After so many months—actually years—and hoping and dreaming of a horse of her own, here she was. And No-Name was more beautiful, and more perfect, than Stevie had ever imagined.

"I told your parents I'd get a picture of this," said Mr. Marsten, climbing out of the front of the station wagon. He raised his camera and managed to catch Stevie at the exact moment she was wiping her eyes.

"Come on over," Stevie said, motioning to Lisa and Carole and Phil. "I want you all in a picture."

Phil stood on the other side of No-Name's head, and Lisa and Carole held up the sign.

"Say cheese," said Mr. Marsten.

They all made silly faces, and No-Name tossed her head at the moment of the photograph.

"Let's try again," Mr. Marsten said, and all of a sudden they all settled into place, Stevie smiling from ear to ear,

Phil smiling at her smile, Lisa and Carole looking at Stevie with pride, and No-Name, with her white exclamation point, looking as if she had been at Pine Hollow for all of her life.

"Show me her stall," Phil said after Mr. Marsten had taken a few more pictures.

"It's in the exclusive district," Stevie said. "Next stall to Starlight."

"That *is* the exclusive district," Phil agreed.

"An empty nameplate," Phil commented as he looked at the blank brass plate next to the stall. "You'll have to fill it soon."

"The wheels are turning already," Stevie said. She led No-Name into the stall and checked, for perhaps the tenth time, to make sure that there was water in the bucket and hay in the bag. She heard the stall door close behind her, and there was Phil.

"The minute I saw you two together, I knew you were right for each other," he said.

"You think so?" Stevie said, sighing, because she had the same feeling. "I feel like No-Name and I will be together forever."

"I know that feeling," Phil said, stepping toward her. He put his hand on Stevie's shoulder, and he was leaning toward her, his eyes half-closed.

As Stevie leaned in for a kiss, she felt something bite

her backside. This wasn't a nibble. It was a genuine bite. "Hey!" she yelled. Phil's eyes popped open with surprise.

Stevie turned to look and remembered that she'd put an apple for No-Name in her back pocket, and now No-Name was trying to get it out by herself.

Stevie dug the apple out of her pocket, put it on her palm, and extended it to No-Name, fingers straight. "Sorry, kid," she said to her, and then over her shoulder to Phil, "I'm really sorry about that."

Outside a horn sounded, and Phil said, "My dad's waiting. I've got to go."

Stevie gave him a rueful smile and said, "Another 'Almost,' I guess."

The horn sounded again, and Phil let himself out through the stall door.

A minute later Lisa and Carole appeared with tack for No-Name. "Max said we can show No-Name around," Carole said. "Starlight is going to introduce her to the trails."

"My own horse," Stevie said dreamily. "I can't believe it. Last Friday it wasn't even a possibility, and now No-Name and I are together."

There was a snort behind her, and Stevie turned to see that No-Name looked definitely annoyed about something.

"What?" Stevie said, turning toward her. "What?"

"I think she wants you to stop talking," Lisa said.

"I think she wants to get out on the trail," Carole said, handing Stevie the bridle.

Stevie rubbed No-Name's exclamation point lovingly, held up the bridle so No-Name could see it, and then slipped it gently into her mouth and then over her ears. As she fastened the chin strap, No-Name was nodding her head, ready to go.

"Let's hit that trail, No-Name."

All of Stevie's worries were gone. This was the best day of her life, and she was going to enjoy every second of it. She couldn't wait to get out on that trail.

"Just one thing, No-Name," she said as she hoisted the saddle and blanket onto her back. "Don't even think about weeds."

ABOUT THE AUTHOR

BONNIE BRYANT is the author of more than sixty books for young readers, including novelizations of movie hits such as *Teenage Mutant Ninja Turtles*® and *Honey, I Blew Up the Kid*, written under her married name, B. B. Hiller.

Ms. Bryant began writing The Saddle Club in 1986. Although she had done some riding before that, she intensified her studies then and found herself learning right along with her characters Stevie, Carole, and Lisa. She claims that they are all much better riders than she is.

Ms. Bryant was born and raised in New York City. She lives in Greenwich Village with her two sons.

We hope you enjoyed reading this book. If you would like to receive further information about available titles in the Bantam series, just write to the following address, with your name and address: Kim Prior, Bantam Books, 61–63 Uxbridge Road, Ealing, London W5 5SA.

If you live in Australia or New Zealand and would like more information about the series, please write to:

Sally Porter
Transworld Publishers
15–25 Helles Avenue
Moorebank
NSW 2170
AUSTRALIA

Kiri Martin
Transworld Publishers (NZ) Ltd
3 William Pickering Drive
Albany
Auckland
NEW ZEALAND